JACKIE CALHOUN

AWAKENINGS

Bella
BOOKS

2012

Bella Books, Inc.
P.O. Box 10543
Tallahassee, FL 32302

Printed in the United States of America on acid-free paper
First published 2012

Editor: Medora McDougall
Cover Designer: Sandy Knowles

ISBN 13: 978-1-59493-305-9

Other Bella Books by Jackie Calhoun

Dedication

In the snow and cold of 2011 thousands upon thousands of Wisconsinites protested in the State Capitol and on the streets of Madison and elsewhere. It was the beginning of an extraordinary recall effort to overcome the conservative tide that blindsided our once progressive state.

I can't rewrite Wisconsin's future, but I can and do salute those who took part in the peaceful demonstrations and the events that followed. As it turned out, I was only able to create the path Sarah and Hayley would take.

About the Author

Jackie Calhoun lives with her partner in northeast Wisconsin. She is the author of twenty-three books. Look for her at www.jackiecalhoun.com or e-mail her at jackie@jackiecalhoun.com or friend her on Facebook.

CHAPTER ONE

February 17, 2011

Sarah

Sarah Sweeney stood in the rotunda of the Wisconsin State Capitol. It was a magnificent building, its interior made up of colorful marble from many different places, stairs and railings that circled up to the fourth balcony. The dome was the epicenter of Madison. Thousands of people stood shoulder-to-shoulder, leaning over the balconies, filling the crosswalks and the rotunda. Outside more marched—an estimated forty thousand in all—carrying signs and chanting, "Kill the bill."

The governor's Budget Repair Bill had brought them here. Made public on February 11, the bill called for, among other things, the end of over fifty years of collective bargaining for nearly 175,000 public employees, including teachers like her. The bill had been put on the fast track for passage. A vote was scheduled that day in the state senate.

As Sarah viewed the throng before her, she zeroed in on a woman emerging from the crowd. The woman's gaze was fixed beyond her shoulder, and Sarah's heart pounded in her ears as the woman's long strides brought her near. She could be no one else, not with that coppery-colored hair bouncing on her shoulders and those pale green eyes. When she was close enough to brush shoulders, Sarah reached out a hand to stop her.

The woman's distracted gaze lit on Sarah. "Excuse me?"

Sarah's fingers tightened on her jacket sleeve. "Hayley?" she said with barely concealed disbelief.

The woman paused and looked at Sarah with equal incredulity before throwing her arms around her. "Sweeney? Sarah? Is it really you?"

Sarah laughed as Hayley picked her up and swung her around before putting her down and holding her at arm's length. "Yeah, it's me, but *I* live in Wisconsin. What are *you* doing here?" She shouted to be heard.

"Writing a story," Hayley yelled in answer. "I had an appointment with one of the Democratic senators, but he's nowhere to be found. You know what's going on?"

Sarah was finding it difficult to believe that her childhood friend and first love was standing here in front of her. "Not with the senator I don't."

They stared at each other for a moment before Hayley said, "Hey, let's go somewhere and talk. I haven't seen you for what? Ten or eleven years?"

"Eleven years," Sarah said, remembering clearly what for her had been a devastating loss. "I can't lose track of my friends, though." She gestured toward Jane Foley, standing next to her. "They're my ride home."

Hayley put an arm around her. "Come on, Sweeney. Excuse us," she said to Jane. "She'll call you." And to Sarah, "You do have a phone, don't you?" Sarah nodded. This was vintage Hayley. She always got her way—at least with Sarah.

Hayley groped for Sarah's hand and pulled her through the throngs of chanting protesters toward the closest exit. Outside, in the cool, sunny winter day, Sarah took up the chant, "Kill the bill," as they threaded their way through the picketers circling the building.

"We can sit out here," she said, dropping the mantra and leading Hayley toward a granite bench halfway down wide stairs. Cold seeped through her jeans when she sat. She looked at Hayley—at her pink cheeks and nose, her bright windblown hair.

Hayley's lips stretched in a smile, revealing straight white teeth, the result of years of braces. "You're really into this, aren't you?"

She tensed. "Of course. Do you realize what's happening here? We're going back to the early twentieth century when workers had no rights."

"I understand." The smile stayed in place. The cat eyes danced with pleasure. The pupils were slits in the pale winter sun.

Sarah took this as thinly disguised laughter. "Think about all the rights you have in the workplace and how you got them." She ticked off on her fingers—"Vacation time, sick leave, forty-hour weeks, health insurance, retirement, unemployment..."

Hayley grabbed her hands. "I know, I know, Sweeney. You don't have to tell me. I'm just so glad to see you."

"No one calls me Sweeney. I don't call you Baxter." She searched Hayley's eyes, looking for the girl she'd fallen in love with all those years ago. Wondering why Hayley hadn't come back looking for her long before this if she was so glad to see her.

"My ass is freezing. Let's go look for a coffee shop."

"We'll never find a place to sit down."

"Come to my hotel. We have coffee there."

Sarah felt a twinge of alarm. "I have to go back inside."

"Hey, I'm not going to let you go. I just found you again."

Her mouth twisted in remembrance. "You let me go a long time ago, Hayley."

Hayley pulled her back down as she tried to stand. "It wasn't like you and I were committed or something."

Sarah stared at her, feeling a stab of long-forgotten pain. "Were you looking for me?" she said, lifting an eyebrow.

"Of course. I called your mom. Did you know I had a huge crush on her when I was a kid?" She grinned again.

Sarah looked into those green eyes and said, "I'm going inside. If you want, you can come with me, but I can't leave." She could not put into words how important it was to her to make a stand on this union-stripping bill—as if one person more out of thousands would make a difference.

Hayley followed her up the steps and through the lines of protesters. "I have a room. You can stay here with me tonight," she said, her warm breath exhaling in Sarah's ear, sending chills up Sarah's neck and into her hair. "That way you can protest tomorrow too, and maybe I'll see the senator."

Sarah's mind homed in on the implications of spending a night with Hayley. She mentally shrugged. It meant she would be here tomorrow. She rang Jane's cell. "I'm staying over with my friend. I haven't seen her in years, and she's got a room. Will you be here tomorrow in case we don't meet up again today?"

"Yes," Jane said. "We'll be taking the shuttle bus back to the parking lot around four. Sure you'll be all right?"

Was she nuts to stay with Hayley and possibly revive all those memories? On the other hand, had anyone even begun to take Hayley's place in her life?

"By the way, it's rumored that the Democratic senators left the state."

"*What*? Are you serious?" Excitement skittered through her, exacting a shiver.

"They don't have a quorum in the senate without at least one Democrat present so they can't vote, not on a budget bill."

Sarah plugged one ear and whooped, "Yoo hoo! No way!"

Jane laughed. "They're buying time. I'll call when I get here tomorrow."

Sarah turned to Hayley. "You can forget about your appointment. They left town."

"Who left town?"

"The Democratic senators. Jane said they went to Illinois so the senate can't vote on the Budget Repair Bill. No quorum."

Hayley stared at her for a moment before her smile spread into a wide grin. "No shit?"

"None." Sarah jumped up and down, whooping again. "Isn't that just great?"

"Yeah, I guess it is. It's a good story. Now can we get that coffee?"

"I'm going to stick around for a while. I don't want to be anywhere else."

Hayley talked to protesters, recording their comments, while Sarah stood among those in the rotunda, joyous with the news that the governor and his party had been thwarted.

***

Hayley's hotel was the only one located on Capitol Square. A Best Western called Inn on the Park, it stood across the street from the Capitol near the corner of Carroll Street. Sarah stuffed her hands in her pockets and hunkered into her down jacket as they crossed the street. Although the week had been unusually warm, there was snow on the ground and when the sun went down, it turned wintry cold.

She was silent as they climbed to the second floor, thinking about what she didn't have—something to sleep in, a toothbrush, clean underwear. She felt more vulnerable with each step.

Hayley slid her card in the slot and the door opened. She dropped her coat on the king-size bed and went straight to the coffeemaker. "Decaf or regular?"

"Decaf," Sarah said. "I have to go out and get a few things if I'm going to spend the night."

"Okay. I saw a Walgreens on the square. We have to eat anyway. I'd like to cruise State Street."

The smell of coffee filled the room, taking away the odor that all hotel rooms seemed to have, at least all the ones Sarah had been in—stale air—maybe because the windows were always closed.

Hayley fished her cell out of her pocket and put it to her ear. "Hi, Kristina. I'm going to be here for a few days. There's a big story in Madison that's spreading to the rest of the nation." She gathered her hair in one hand and shook it out, thick and tangled. She had always had great hair.

Sarah went to the bathroom and shut the door. She peed and, while washing her hands, she stared in the mirror. Her blue-green eyes were watery from the cold, her reddish-blond hair seriously matted by the knit cap she'd worn, her fair skin burned from exposure to the wind. She ran her fingers through the hair, giving it a lift, and returned to the room.

Hayley was still on the phone, pacing as she talked. "Gotta go. Talk to you tomorrow." She flipped the phone shut and slid it into her pocket, then handed a cup of coffee to Sarah. "This'll heat you up."

"Thanks. Actually, it's not a cold week. We're lucky." She warmed her hands on the cup as she sipped.

"I'll bet you're tired. I'm going to stretch out. Care to join me?"

Instead, she chose to sit in one of the chairs by the window.

Hayley threw herself on the bed and sighed. She extracted her cell phone from her pocket, looked at the display, and tossed it on the spread. "Want to catch up?"

She shrugged, reluctant to start. "You go first."

"I moved to New York after graduation." Hayley covered her eyes with a hand and wiped her face. "I'd been offered a job. I was so busy, Sarah. I just lost myself in that little newspaper. I had to live with someone to afford living there at all. She was much older than I, and when we became lovers, I was too ashamed to tell you. I came home when I knew you wouldn't be at the lake."

Stunned by the unexpected admission, Sarah thought it sounded like a half-assed apology. She wasn't sure she wanted to hear Hayley's life story after she lost track of her. She jumped to her feet, but she wasn't quick enough. Hayley blocked her way to the door. Besides, where would she go?

"Hey, this is all old stuff, Sarah. Constance and I fell apart when she took up with someone even younger than I was, and I moved in with my friend, Kristina. My life is in New York. Yours is here. I didn't want to start something that couldn't go anywhere." She leaned against the door, arms crossed, a crooked smile plastered on her face. "I carried you around in my mind, though—your hair blazing in the summer sun, your eyes a reflection of the lake, your nose always peeling."

If anything, Hayley's words made her angrier. They rang untrue. "When you never answered my messages, I went to your house to find out if you were alive. Your mom said you'd abandoned them too."

"You know how that is. Constance is eighteen years older than I am, two years younger than my mom. My mom's not like yours. She never would have understood."

"What mine wouldn't understand is why you never contacted me." Of course, her mother hadn't actually known what had gone on between Hayley and her those last three summers. Even if she had guessed, she never would have realized the extent of their love affair.

The summer Hayley stopped coming home Sarah's mom had been so distracted. She'd been coming out herself and her brother, Sarah's uncle, had been terribly sick with AIDS. Sarah was sure she'd hardly registered on her mother's radar screen. Even thinking about that time brought the pain back, the sense of loss and abandonment.

"Look, I'm sorry. I can't tell you how much. I loved you."

Sarah's hands curled into fists. She whispered. "You don't just drop someone you love."

Hayley raised her eyebrows in that infuriating way she had when she was sure she was right. "Yeah, you do, when you think you're never coming back."

The anger drained away. She'd probably never see Hayley again. She plopped back down in the chair. "It's okay. It doesn't matter anyway. It was a long time ago."

Hayley dropped onto the bed again. "Tell me about yourself."

Sarah waved a hand. "There's not much to tell."

"Are you with someone?"

"Nope. I live alone."

Hayley yawned hugely, which annoyed Sarah even more. "Sorry. I can't believe you aren't with anyone. You're so cute."

She laughed dismissively. Hayley was a hopeless flatterer. "Want to go out to eat?" She had to get away from this conversation. Her relationships had seriously sucked. The one with James had been a mistaken attempt to be socially correct. The other with Molly had lasted about five years, till she had cheated on Sarah with one of their friends. She'd convinced herself it hadn't hurt all that much, and then she had wondered if she was somehow lacking in passion.

"What I want is for you to come here and pretend the bed is a beach and we're lying on it. Like old times."

Sarah stared at her. Was she so dense she couldn't see or understand Sarah's anger, or was she so sure of herself she thought sex would make everything all right? She stood up. "I'm going to Walgreens and then find something to eat."

"I'm going with you."

CHAPTER TWO

Summer 1997

It was the first summer that Sarah's sister and brother weren't going with her and her mother to the lake. Beth had a job at the mall, and Jeff was playing in a baseball league. They were coming with their dad in August. Sarah had graduated from Whitmore High in May and had been doing odd jobs for her father's law firm. He had let her go because there wasn't enough to keep her busy.

Her mother had taken a break from the newspaper where she wrote an advice column. She'd said that she had answered enough letters to fill her column for at least two months and was taking a bunch with her to keep her busy while she was gone.

"Do you want me to drive?" Sarah asked as they sped north on Highway 41.

"I'm okay." Her mom flashed Sarah a smile. She loved going to their summer place. The whole family did, except for maybe her dad, who seemed to grow restless after a few days. Sarah's mother's parents had owned the place originally. When they died, they'd left it to their son and daughter.

Sarah was the child who looked most like her mother, with blue-green eyes and reddish-blond hair and fair skin. She leaned into the door and dreamily stared out the window. Hayley was on her mind. Would she have a job? Would she be disappointed that Beth hadn't come with Sarah and her mom? Would she be as excited to see Sarah as Sarah would be to see her?

Hayley lived on the back road, where lake access meant fifty feet of beach at the end of a two-rut sand road about a quarter mile from Sarah's place. Everyone called this little piece of beach the public landing.

After they bumped down their own sandy driveway and carried suitcases and coolers inside, Sarah called Hayley's home and left a message on the answering machine. Then while her mom put the food away, she threw open windows to let in the smell of lake and pines. She changed into her swimsuit in her upstairs bedroom and came back with a beach towel around her neck.

"Go on down to the lake. I'll come as soon as I finish putting a few things away up here," her mom said with a smile.

Sarah hurried down the steps to the lake. It was a hot, windy day, the kind she loved. After dropping her towel on the pier, she walked into the water. The heavy liquid closed around her. When she could no longer feel the sandy bottom, she began treading water. Her heart jumped as she looked down the lake toward the public beach. The raft there was rocking wildly as those on it jumped off and climbed back on. She stuck an arm out of the water and waved. Someone waved back and yelled her name.

She spit out a stream of water and began swimming. When she reached the raft and climbed the ladder, Hayley's brother, Mike, tried to push her off. Before he could do so, she flopped backward and got a snoot full. When she popped through the surface, a grinning Hayley was treading water next to her.

"It's about time you got here, Sweeney. Let's go to your place. These guys are so juvenile," Hayley said as if they'd just seen each other yesterday instead of last August. They swam to shore, where Hayley grabbed a beach towel lying on an overturned boat and threw it over both their shoulders. "You're gonna burn, you know."

"Hey, come back," Mike yelled. "I'm sorry. I was just saying hello."

Sarah waved a hand in his direction and smiled. Nothing had changed. "Later," she hollered.

The previous summer she had gotten seriously sunburned when she and Hayley and Beth swam around the lake. The skin on her shoulders had blistered and peeled, and for a week she'd let no one near her, lest they touch her. She was surprised Hayley remembered.

Hayley was wearing the same skimpy bikini she'd worn last year, but now she filled it to overflowing. Her breasts mounded out of the bra like risen bread, and the bottom barely covered her ass. "I know," she said, meeting Sarah's gaze. "I need a new suit."

Sarah replied wistfully, "No, no. I'm just envious."

Hayley grinned, her pupils pinpoints encircled by light green irises. "Yeah? I don't look fat?"

"You're not fat." And she wasn't. She was just right.

"I thought you'd never get here."

"Me too. I left a message for you."

"Where's Beth?"

"She has a job and Jeff is obsessed with his baseball league. They're coming in August with Dad. I'm here with Mom." Hayley smelled of suntan lotion—cocoa butter. Her shoulder and hip bumped against Sarah's as they walked.

"I quit my job. Don't tell my parents, though."

"I quit mine too. I was working for my dad. It was mind-numbing. I'll never be a lawyer." The sand had soaked up the heat of the day, and as she stepped into the water to cool her feet, a frog jumped out of the way.

"Move over." Hayley waded in next to her. "I quit my job to be with you." She turned her head and smiled at Sarah.

Sarah didn't question her feelings for Hayley. She just figured all best friends commanded this fierce love. "Me too. I couldn't wait to get here."

"Can I stay over?" Hayley asked, slipping an arm around Sarah's waist.

Sarah's heart soared. If it were up to her, Hayley would move in.

"Let's ask your mom."

Her mother looked up as they approached. "Hi, Hayley."

"Hi, Mrs. S. What are you reading?"

"*Angela's Ashes.*" She raised the book so that Hayley could read the title.

"Did you ever read *Follow the River*?" They were big readers, her mom and Hayley, as was she.

"I did. That was a good book." Her mother looked up from under a floppy hat, her eyes hidden behind large sunglasses.

"I don't know if I would have survived," Hayley said.

Sarah settled on the lounge chair next to her mom and patted the leg rest. Hayley sat down and relinquished the beach towel to Sarah. Hayley already had a deep tan.

"It must have been difficult, straddling both worlds," Sarah's mom said.

"I suppose. It was a good read." Hayley toed the sand. They were still talking about *Follow the River*.

"Mom, is it okay if Hayley stays over tonight?" Sarah was watching a skier. Water sprayed from beneath the one ski in a long arc as he skimmed the waves. The skier straightened and sped across the boat's wake to do the same on the other side. She wished she could ski like that, but they had no speedboat, just a fiberglass rowboat with a ten-horse power motor.

"Of course. What are your school plans, Hayley?" her mom asked.

"I've got a full scholarship to Brown." A smile split Hayley's face.

"Congratulations!" Sarah's mom said. "I'm impressed."

Sarah was startled out of lethargy. She knew nothing about this scholarship. She thought Hayley was headed for UW-Madison as she was and they were going to room together.

"What?" she asked, her heart pounding with dismay.

"Hey, you can come visit." She placed a warm hand on Sarah's leg.

Sarah jerked away, her eyes suddenly hot with tears.

"Let's go get my stuff, Sarah."

Unable to meet anyone's gaze, she stared at the boathouse, remembering how they'd played cards inside—she and Hayley and Beth and sometimes Jeff and Mike—with the doors open and the rain sluicing down so hard it turned the lake into a boil. The betrayal made her feel vulnerable.

"Hey, wake up." Hayley shook her arm.

Again she pulled away. "I'll stay here. You go."

"Come on, Sarah," Hayley pleaded.

Because her mother was watching, she went. They walked down the long driveway toward the back road. It was windless away from the lake and hotter.

"I couldn't turn it down, Sweeney. I wasn't offered a scholarship from Madison." She slipped her fingers between Sarah's, but Sarah's hand remained limp.

She was afraid if she said anything she'd start crying and not stop. Her chest was tight and her throat hurt.

"I'm sorry." Hayley kicked the sand underfoot. "What do you want me to say? Are you going to spoil the whole goddamn summer by sulking?"

Sarah spun around and started back toward the house. She began to run, sprinting as if she could outrun the pain. When she stepped on a pinecone, she grabbed her foot and hopped up and down. She was crying now—hard.

Hayley caught up with her. "I wouldn't have done it if I'd known you cared so much."

Sarah dropped her foot and hissed, "Yes, you would."

"I'm going to get my stuff." Hayley walked away.

Sarah continued the other way, still crying. She would have hidden among the white pines lining the driveway but for the patches of poison ivy along the side of the road. Instead, she went to her room and threw herself on the bed. After a while, she fell asleep.

Her mother wakened her. She stood next to the bed in shorts and a T-shirt. "That came as a surprise to me too."

She rolled onto her back, her arm over her eyes. In the fifth grade her best friend had moved to California. It was something she'd thought she couldn't bear, but she couldn't change it either. She'd thrown herself into her mother's arms and wept inconsolably. She longed to do that now, but she wasn't ten years old anymore.

"I guess we should be happy for her. Brown is a good school." Her mother sat on the bed next to her. "Remember when Caroline moved to California?"

Sometimes her mother uncannily guessed what she was thinking. It was kind of scary. "I know. I found another best friend." But what she felt for Hayley was different. She couldn't put a finger on it, couldn't give it a name, but she knew her attachment to Hayley was more than a friendship.

"Aren't you hungry? There is leftover potato salad in the fridge, and I warmed the baked ham." Her mom pushed Sarah's damp hair back from her forehead, her touch tentative as if she feared Sarah would turn away.

Sarah loved her mom's potato salad. She hadn't eaten lunch, and she thought maybe the sickness in her stomach was caused by hunger. As much as she would like to waste away and maybe make Hayley change her mind, she knew her body would never let her do it. "Okay. Thanks."

"Hayley is downstairs. Are you coming down?"

She felt panicky and rolled away, so her mother wouldn't see her face. She knew she was overreacting. "I'll come down when she's gone."

However, Hayley was no longer downstairs. She spoke from the doorway. "I knew you'd say that. I'm going to stay here until you talk to me."

"You know what?" her mom said. "I'm going down to the lake. You two can deal with this without me. It's too nice out to be inside." Her mom left, pattering barefoot down the stairs and out the door, the screen slapping shut behind her in the quiet of the moment.

Hayley sat next to her. "You're my best friend, Sarah. I love you."

Sarah scoffed and said, "If that was true..." and Hayley shut her up with a kiss on the mouth. It stopped the words, and her heart went crazy, taking her breath with it. When Hayley's tongue touched hers, she remembered her mother. Maybe she had come back inside and was climbing the stairs right now. She broke away, panting and struggling to get out from under Hayley.

Hayley rolled off her and rested her head on her hand, her fingers in the thickness of her hair. "Didn't you like it?"

"I never kissed a girl," she mumbled. She'd gone with Tim Foster her senior year. He had groped her, and she had let him whenever they were alone in his car.

"Me neither," she said. "I went with Bobby Tiercel last year. Remember, I told you about Bobby? You were going out with someone too."

"Yeah, I was." Wasn't that what she was supposed to do? Go out with guys?

"Did you do it with him?" Hayley asked.

Her eyes felt like hot holes in the flush of her face. "No. Not all the way. Did you?"

"Yeah, and I'd like to do it with you. It'll be better with you."

Sarah rolled off the bed onto her feet. "I'm going to get something to eat and go for a swim." She still had her suit on.

"I brought my stuff, so I can stay overnight," Hayley said.

She paused, her back to Hayley, and then continued out of the room. She wasn't sure she could stand this kind of excitement or the pain that went with it.

With plates of ham sandwiches and potato salad she and Hayley walked down to the lake. Sarah's mom was sitting on the pier, her feet dangling in the water. The sun hung low in the west, flanked by a few thin pink clouds.

Afraid her mother would be able to tell what had happened by looking at her, Sarah plunked down in a beach chair. She was a jumble of feelings—doubt, shame, fear, dismay—all wrapped in such excitement that she couldn't sit. She set the plate down and ran into the water. At waist level, she dove and swam away from the shore.

Her mother's voice reached her, calling as she had when Sarah was a child. "Don't go out too far."

The boat bumped her, startling her. She looked up to see Hayley wriggle out of her T-shirt and dive into the lake. The craft rocked and drifted toward shore. Sarah was watching it when Hayley pulled her under and kissed her again before they both exploded through the surface.

"Hey," Sarah said in protest.

Hayley moved close so that their bodies touched under the water where they bobbed, face to face. She searched Sarah's eyes. "You liked it."

"I can't..." Sarah began, looking into the pale green eyes, then quickly realized she could, and it seemed as if all the years of their friendship had led to this moment and she'd always known it. She backstroked away from Hayley. "Not now, not here."

"Later," Hayley said, "when we go to bed."

They retrieved the boat and pulled it up on the beach next to the boathouse. Hayley took her plate out on the pier and sat next to Sarah's mother. She patted the boards beside her, but Sarah plopped in a beach chair and started to read her mom's book, taking bites of food.

The light was disappearing from the sky, leaving a crimson smudge along the horizon. She had gotten too much sun and was now cold. They all went inside and Hayley followed her upstairs. Sarah took her clothes into the bathroom to change.

The three of them played cards on the porch, but after an hour, her mom wanted to read and went to bed with her book.

"Let's go see what your brother is doing," Sarah said. "It's too early to go to bed."

Hayley shrugged. "Sure." They walked along the lake's edge to the public landing, where Hayley's sixteen-year-old brother and a couple of other guys had lit a small fire. Lightning bugs flashed on and off along the shore, lighting up the grass and bushes. A strong sweet-smelling plant filled her senses, and her ears tuned into a chorus of frogs singing loudly from a nearby marsh. She had to pause and take it all in. This was where she felt most alive.

"What's in the bag?" Hayley asked as they sat in the sand.

"Beer," Mike said, handing the bottle to Hayley.

"It's warm," she said, taking a drink and passing the bottle to Sarah.

Sarah swallowed. "Yuck. That's bad."

"You go with what you got. Don't drink it if you don't want it."

One of Mike's friends, who looked familiar, was now swigging out of the bottle. The small fire crackled like fireworks. "Hey, Sarah," Mike said. "You back for the summer?"

"Yeah." She wrapped her arms around her legs and dug her bare toes into the now cool sand. Under the surface it felt damp and dense.

When the bottle was empty, Mike retrieved another from the lake where it was supposedly staying cool. After a few drinks, the beer didn't taste so bad. She leaned back on her hands. The stars flung across the dark sky floated on the lake. Voices carried over the water, along with the laughter and shouts of kids swimming.

She and Hayley walked back to the house and tiptoed across the plank floors. Her mother's door was closed and the interior of the house dark except for a light over the kitchen sink, which Sarah turned off. She dropped her shorts on the floor of her bedroom and took her bra off under her shirt, wriggling out of it. In bed she hugged her side, the one facing the window, and turned her back to Hayley. The smell of the lake drifted through the screen, and she fell into a beer-soaked sleep.

She awoke sodden from a dream to the feel of Hayley's hand between her legs. Cicadas buzzed loudly outside the open window. She froze, feigning sleep, thinking if she was passive she could remain somehow uninvolved and innocent. But when she shuddered, Hayley grabbed her shoulder and pulled her onto her back.

"Hey, I know you're awake. Do you know you're a tease?" She leaned over Sarah, her long hair falling around Sarah's face, tickling her. Her breath smelled of beer. "Come on. You have to return the favor," she said, kissing Sarah hard.

The room was so dark she could hardly make out Hayley's features. It was as if she was still in a dream, making out with Tim, who had morphed into Hayley. When Hayley took her hand and put it between her legs, she was surprised by lust. She'd been fooling herself. It wasn't Tim or any boy she wanted. It was Hayley.

In a moment of sisterly intimacy, Beth had told her how to please herself. Now Sarah did to Hayley what she did to herself, and Hayley writhed under her touch. At one point she whispered,

"Shhh." She could see better now. Hayley's head was thrown back, exposing her slender neck and the pulsing artery in it. Sarah kissed the warm skin, and Hayley's body went into spasms.

After, they lay side by side, damp from the heat. Their shoulders, arms, hips and legs stuck together. Wide-awake, Sarah stared at the ceiling. It hadn't fallen on her. She laughed to herself and turned her face toward Hayley, who gave her another kiss.

"I love you, Sweeney."

"I love you, Baxter." She threaded her fingers in the thickness of Hayley's hair. "You are so brave."

"And you didn't want to do it."

"I was scared. Aren't you? Aren't we those girls the guys make fun of, the ones who say all we need is a good fuck?"

"Who cares what they say? Who is going to know anyway?"

CHAPTER THREE

February 2011

State Street was crowded. They ordered a half veggie, half pepperoni pizza and took it to the hotel, along with a six-pack of Leinie's Red. Hayley set the pizza on the table, and Sarah opened a couple of beers. Outside, scores of people milled around Capitol Square. Many had moved inside and were sleeping on the marble floor. A medic station, child day care, a food court and sleeping quarters were in place. These amenities along with hundreds of signs, banners and live music created a sense of camaraderie and purpose.

"How's your mom?" Hayley asked as she took a big bite out

of a slice on the pepperoni side. She moaned and wiped her chin. "I am *so* hungry." She looked at Sarah expectantly.

Sarah remembered Hayley's surprise admission of a childhood crush on her mother and said tersely, "Mom's fine. She's living at the lake now."

"My mother said your parents got a divorce."

"A long time ago." The summer Hayley hadn't come home.

Hayley's pale green eyes bored into her. "Is this some big secret?" She had always pried Sarah's secrets out of her—with a look, with a question—as if she had a right to know.

Sarah dug in her heels. "A lot of things happened."

"Look, I'm sorry about the divorce. Sorry I wasn't there for you." Hayley leaned forward, elbows on the table, her face and tone serious.

"I survived. I now have a stepmother who's young enough to be my sister." She spoke with irony.

"That must be weird. I don't remember your dad very well. Tell me about your mom."

"It was tough for her that summer." She remembered her mother worrying about Uncle Gordie and at the same time lighting up like a torch whenever Pat Thompson showed up.

"How tough?"

She unexpectedly began to tear up and mumbled something about having to go. But before she could lock the bathroom door, Hayley shoved through it behind her.

"What the hell?" she said, putting her arms around Sarah from behind. "Hey, whatever it is, it was a long time ago," she whispered in Sarah's ear.

Sarah's vision cleared. She sniffed. "Let go," she said calmly. "I'm all right."

Hayley released her grip and retreated, shutting Sarah in the bathroom.

Sarah blew her nose and looked in the mirror. She was a mess. What could Hayley possibly see in her? After she peed, she splashed water on her face and tried to fluff up her hair, but it seemed to have died on her.

Hayley was waiting at the table. "I always feel better after I'm fed. Help me here. I can't eat and drink all this alone," she said, although she had devoured nearly half the pizza and drunk two beers.

When they finished off the food and beer, Hayley suggested they go to bed. "It's always easier to talk in the dark."

The resistance went out of Sarah. She had been up since before six and was exhausted emotionally and physically. She went into the bathroom to change into the T-shirt she'd bought to sleep in—black cotton, made in China. She thought the color would hide what was underneath.

When she switched off the bathroom light, both rooms turned into a cave and she groped her way along the wall till she found the bed and Hayley's feet. She crawled onto the other side and lay down near the edge. The pillow was fat and hard. As she had that first time at the lake all those years ago, she turned her back to Hayley. It seemed as if she was stuck in the past.

"What is Mike doing?" she asked.

"He's a civil engineer. He works for the Wisconsin Department of Transportation."

Lying there not able to see was disorienting. After a while, she realized Hayley had fallen asleep. Both disappointed and relieved, she relaxed enough to drift off too.

***

She awoke to a shaft of daylight peeking through the slightly open drapes. Before she turned over, she knew Hayley was not in the bed. The sound of water gushing suddenly stopped, and a few minutes later, Hayley came out of the bathroom wrapped in a towel. She rummaged around in her suitcase, while Sarah tried to keep her eyes off her backside.

When Hayley dropped the towel, Sarah got out of bed, grabbed her clothes and headed toward the bathroom. The water felt deliciously warm. She washed her hair and body quickly, and when she stepped out onto the mat, Hayley was knocking on the door.

"Just a minute," she called, pulling her clothes over her still damp skin before flipping off the lock.

"Sweeney, I know every inch of you. You don't need to hide."

"I'm not hiding," she said.

Hayley laughed. "I won't make a move without your permission. Promise."

"Okay. Quit calling me Sweeney." She started toward the door. Hayley stopped her with a big kiss.

"You lied," Sarah said, rubbing a hand over her mouth.

"That's how it all started. Remember? I caught you off guard." She looked serious for a moment and then shrugged. "You're as safe as you want to be."

In the lobby they poured coffee into Styrofoam cups. "Let's go somewhere and get a real coffee and a bagel," Hayley said, and they went out into the streets where protesters were already milling around. The weather was still unseasonably warm, and they walked down King Street to a small café, where they bought bagels with cream cheese and coffee in big mugs and sat down near the windows.

Hayley licked a bit of white stuff off her lips. She had a great mouth, full and wide, and when she caught Sarah looking at it, she said, "What if I tell you what I know?"

Sarah sipped at the steaming coffee, feeling its heat seep into her stomach and spread outside its walls. "I'm listening."

"Your mom lives with a woman, and your uncle died of AIDS."

A frown etched itself between Sarah's eyebrows. "Can you imagine what it was like for Mom that summer, for all of us?" She remembered her uncle—gaunt and breathless with bleeds showing through his skin like purple birthmarks gone wild. Even so, he had kept his sense of humor. Her mom had been frantic for everyone's safety because some crazy homophobe was making threats. Pat had been her mom's mainstay. Sarah and Beth and Jeff were her mom's chief worries. She was desperate for them to leave so they would be safe. And as if all of this weren't enough, Sarah hadn't seen or heard from Hayley. It had felt as if the people she loved most had abandoned her.

"No. Tell me." The babble of voices at the nearby tables faded.

"Remember the women Jeff called the dykes?" Hayley nodded. "Well, Mom's partner is one of those women—Pat Thompson. She's younger than Mom but not near as young as Dad's wife."

"And your uncle?" Hayley asked, her expression a mask of concern.

"He turned up the summer before, remember, with his partner, Brad? I hardly saw my uncle until then. They were both so much fun, but Brad died of AIDS that fall or maybe it was winter, and then Gordie died the next summer at the lake." Tears teetered on her eyelids, and she blinked, annoyed with herself. She rarely cried, and now it was like she'd lost all control.

Chin in both hands, Hayley seemed to have forgotten her coffee and bagel. "And then what happened?"

"Mom just sort of retreated and after enough months passed, she and Pat moved in together. Pat is a retired teacher."

"No wonder I fell in love with your mom." She looked kind of dreamy eyed.

"And here I thought I was the reason you hung around," she said with some annoyance.

Hayley gave her a sad sort of smile. "You were, but I had places to go and I went. I couldn't see any other future at the time."

"Yeah, well, you always were more adventurous." She finished her bagel. She had written off Hayley a long time ago.

"Want another cup of coffee?"

"No. It'll just make me pee."

"What do you teach?"

"American lit and composition."

"Do you like teaching?"

"I do. The public schools are going to lose funding. We know that much. The governor says the state is broke, but what is more important than education? Our students are already way behind those in the industrialized world. How can we compete for jobs?"

"I don't remember you being so serious, Sarah," Hayley said.

"This is serious. This is my life." She didn't like people who had no sense of humor. Had she lost hers?

"Will you stay another night? I have to go home Sunday."

She looked away, knowing she would, not wanting to show any eagerness. She felt so vulnerable, so needy. Hayley had always made her feel that way. "Do you like what you do?"

"Love it. Read my blog." Hayley picked up her bagel and began to eat.

Even though it was warm for February, the morning air held a chill. The shuttles from the malls near the beltway were arriving. People spilled out of them onto Wisconsin Avenue and funneled into Capitol Square, waving signs, already chanting— "Union busting." She began shouting with them.

Someone with a battery-powered megaphone yelled, "What does democracy look like?" and the crowd roared, "This is what democracy looks like."

Hayley put an arm around her and squeezed. "You are such an activist."

Again she felt that Hayley was patronizing her, and she shook free. It wasn't only the attempt to do away with fifty years of public unions that had drawn her here. It was taking health care out from under the oversight of the legislature and giving it to an administrator, a man who'd said he didn't believe in Medicare or Senior Care, a man who would only answer to the governor. It was also the proposal to sell state-owned heating plants without bids.

Ultimately, it was the power grab that had aroused tens of thousands of people enough to demonstrate in the cold, the wind and snow of winter. The protesters had eschewed violence. Instead, everyone was friendly. They were allies in this fight.

After walking around the square a few times, and it was a huge square, they climbed one set of steps to the Capitol. At the upper level was a wide walkway around the building. Here too protesters marched, carrying signs. Speakers were set up, ready for the rally to begin. They climbed more steps and entered the building.

Inside, chanting made ordinary conversation impossible. The atmosphere was electric, thousands of people united. She shouted with the others till her voice petered out. Protesters crowded the rotunda, the balconies and hallways.

Hayley had been taking pictures, blindly focusing with one arm raised. She stuck to Sarah like Velcro. As they paused at the edge of the crowd on the second floor next to the railing around the rotunda, Hayley suggested they exchange cell numbers in case they were inadvertently separated.

That reminded Sarah to call Jane. "Where are you?"

"In the shuttle bus. Where are you?"

"In the Capitol. I'm staying another night. Are you coming again on Saturday?"

"Yes. Listen, if we don't meet up today, let's do it tomorrow. Okay?"

"My mom is coming tomorrow."

"Call me anyway. I hear it's going to be huge."

"I hope so." It was hard to keep track of more than two people in the milling crowds. She looked around for Hayley, who was right behind her.

"Don't worry. I won't lose you. I just found you again."

She nodded. "I could sleep inside here, like all these other people are doing."

"On marble floors. That would be fun." Hayley's pale green eyes glittered, her mouth twitched.

"I think that probably is exciting."

Hayley's eyebrows shot up. "More exciting than sleeping with me?"

Sarah knew no one could hear them. She smiled thinly and began working her way through the crowd, trusting that Hayley was on her heels.

She hooked up with Jane Foley and Margaret Dempson, a math teacher, on the veranda. Sarah spotted them as they emerged from the crowds circling the building. She yelled and waved an arm.

Jane grinned at her. "No school yesterday and today. Not enough teachers."

Sarah introduced Hayley as a childhood friend who was here from New York to write about the protests.

Jane jumped right in as if being interviewed. "I am so impressed by the organization. Shuttle buses, the unions grilling brats and passing them out free, the Teamsters' semi trucks parked on the square, the porta-potties. And the peacefulness of it all, that too is impressive."

"The firefighters and police are the only public employees allowed to keep their collective bargaining rights, and they're here protesting with us. Who would have thought?" Margaret said. "The governor has awakened the unions. We should be thanking him."

"Can I quote you?" Hayley asked. "I like the awakening bit."

"Sure. It's true." Margaret was short and shapely with hacked-off gray hair that somehow looked good on her.

Jane was tall with brown, curly hair and dark eyes behind wire-rimmed glasses. She was one of Sarah's best friends, although Sarah had never confided that she was a lesbian. Was it possible to have a best friend who didn't know you were gay? She sometimes wondered.

They joined the people on the street for a while, taking in the signs. Sarah's favorites were the shapes of Wisconsin as a fist. The yellow background, black print and fist had "Solidarity" printed on it, while the "Stand For Wisconsin" signs were red with blue fists. A small band of drummers marched past. Whenever someone shouted in protest, they all joined in. After about five more laps around the Capitol, they went back inside and merged with the roaring crowds.

Around four, Jane and Margaret left to catch a shuttle. The next day they were coming down on one of the buses hired by the unions to ferry people to Madison and back. Sarah briefly considered going with them, knowing even as she did that she wouldn't leave. She and Hayley crossed Capitol Square to the hotel. The street was closed to traffic.

Except for the underwear she had purchased, she'd been wearing the same clothes for two days. Her long underwear shirt felt like a second skin. The hotel enclosed her in its sterile warmth. In the room she hung her jacket on the clothes rack inside the door.

Hayley shrugged out of hers and threw it on the bed. She fished her cell out of her pocket and put it to her ear. "'Lo. What's up?" There was a pause before Hayley said with annoyance, "I was going to stay through Sunday." Another pause. "Okay, okay. But I'm coming back next weekend." A short silence followed. "Yeah. Me too." She tossed the phone on her coat.

"Me too" was usually what you said when the person on the other end of the line said he or she loved or missed you. Kristina must be more than a roommate. Sarah was fooling herself if she thought Hayley wasn't involved with someone. Hayley had always been a sexual person. She threw herself on the chair nearest the window and stared out at the Capitol and the many people still surrounding it.

Hayley said, "I have to go home tomorrow afternoon. Will your friends be back?"

"Mom and Pat are coming tomorrow. I can always hitch a ride home with them."

"Why didn't you tell me your mom is coming?" A smile stretched Hayley's mouth wide.

She shrugged. "I figured you'd find out when she got here."

"Wow!" Hayley said, falling into the other chair. "I can't wait to see her."

Sarah felt a twinge of jealousy. When had her mother become a hot commodity? "You're leaving."

"Not till late."

"I'm hungry," she said.

"Where do you want to go?"

"I don't know. Someplace cheap."

"You'll stay with me next weekend, won't you, if this is still going on?" Hayley looked intently at her.

"It will be and I already said I would." Sarah flushed under the blunt gaze. "I'll keep coming back till it's over."

"Do you think there's a chance to change things? I mean, don't the Republicans control both chambers and the governor's office? How can you win?"

"We can change the minds of some, if there are enough of us." She sounded more positive than she felt, but there was nothing to do but go forward.

"Seems to me this governor is just going to push his agenda on through," Hayley said. She stood up. "Let's go eat. I'm buying."

"You bought last night. It's my turn."

"You always were stubborn."

Was she? She wasn't going to let Hayley pay her way, though, so that she felt she owed her. She was stubborn about that.

Hayley hustled her into her jacket.

"Wait. I have to use the bathroom." The skin on her face looked raw in the mirror, especially her nose. Lovely, she thought. She hadn't taken the knit hat off this time. Maybe she would sleep in it.

Outside, protesters hung around with signs slung over their shoulders or tucked under their arms. State Street was crowded with people standing in doorways waiting to get into restaurants.

Smells of bread and sautéed garlic and onions drifted through open doors. When they finally ate, it was after eight thirty. They filled plates from a buffet and found a small table in a far corner. The Greek salad was limp, the bread crusty and dry, but Sarah devoured the food quickly and went back for baklava. She guzzled two glasses of water.

Hayley ate chicken wrapped in filo pastry. "Are you ready?" she said when there was nothing more on either of their plates. She did not argue when Sarah paid with her debit card.

The night felt less cold with food in her stomach, Sarah realized as they walked back toward the hotel. She was tired from being outside, from walking for what seemed endless miles, from the excitement of being a part of something so much bigger than she was.

At the hotel, Hayley sat down at the small table with her laptop and began to type. Sarah went into the bathroom and took a hot shower. She washed her hair and blew it dry. When she came out, Hayley was still at the computer, so she climbed into bed.

"Is the light going to bother you?" Hayley asked without looking up.

"No." She had bought *The Girl Who Played with Fire* at Walgreens the night before, having read the first book in the trilogy, but she'd been too distracted to start it. Now she cracked it open and began to read and was still reading more than an hour later. When Hayley shut her laptop and went into the bathroom, she put the book down and turned toward the draped window. She heard the spurt of the shower, but she never heard Hayley come to bed.

When Sarah woke in the night, Hayley was tucked up behind her, one arm thrown across her ribs. The heat from her body radiated through Sarah. There was nowhere to go. She lay on the edge of the bed, curled like a snail into a shell.

She gave Hayley a nudge. "You're hogging the bed."

"You are such a hardnose," Hayley whispered into her ear. "Why pretend you don't want it when you do?"

Was that what she was doing? Sort of, maybe, but Hayley not only lived a thousand miles away, she lived with a woman. "You already have a lover," she murmured.

"Who?" Hayley asked sleepily.

"Kristina?" she answered, less sure of herself.

Hayley laughed, a deep-throated chuckle. "Kristina is married."

She turned onto her back to see the truth. Hayley brushed the hair off her face and kissed her. "It's torture to lie in bed with you," she said softly. "Is it not the same for you? Do you remember how we were always looking for a place to make love? We don't have to hide anymore." She stroked Sarah's side, her thumb brushing against Sarah's breast.

Paralyzed by desire, Sarah closed her eyes as if in denial, but her back arched ever so slightly.

"Look at me, Sarah."

Hayley's pupils were huge. Her hand moved down the outside of Sarah's thigh and up the inside. Sarah trembled. A small moan escaped her as Hayley leaned over and put her hot, wet mouth on her nipple. Hayley laughed softly and covered Sarah's crotch with her hand, and Sarah felt an embarrassing gush of fluid.

She gave up all resistance and responded with the passion she'd stored up over the years. Afterward they lay panting among the tangle of sheets that had pulled free. Sarah tingled all over. "Who taught you to do it that way?"

"Head to toe? Exquisite, isn't it? We never thought of such things when we were kids."

Sarah hadn't thought of it until now. "Constance?" she guessed as Hayley wrapped her in her arms.

"Does it matter?"

They spent the night fitted together front to back, turning as one, covers thrown back against the heat their bodies produced.

The next morning Sarah went quietly to the bathroom, where she peed and brushed her teeth. When she returned to the bed, Hayley was awake.

"I've already been to the bathroom." Hayley took Sarah's face between her hands and kissed her teasingly. "How about a repeat of last night's performance? You were spectacular."

But Sarah thought it was Hayley who had been the star.

***

When Hayley checked out that morning, Sarah called her mom. She pictured her fumbling for her phone, which was never at hand, as she waited through five rings.

"Hi, sweetie. We're at the East Towne Mall, waiting for the shuttle."

"I have a surprise for you."

"Hayley? She called me a few days ago, asking about you. How is she?"

"Fantastic" came to mind, but she squelched it. "Much the same."

"The bus is here. I'll call when we get downtown."

Hayley left her bag at the front desk for later pick up and turned to Sarah. "Let's go to that coffee shop."

Already protesters were pouring off the buses on Wisconsin Avenue and heading toward Capitol Square. The two young women moved against the flow and ducked into the café on King Street. A line had formed inside. Sarah got a table while Hayley shuffled forward and ordered two cups of coffee and bagels with cream cheese, which she carried to where Sarah was waiting.

Sarah's anger had vanished after a night of sex. What did that say about her? That she was a pushover? Hayley had dumped her eleven years ago without any explanation. And now, after one night of intimacy, she was ready to forgive. She would never forget, though, nor would she ever be so trusting again.

When Hayley answered her phone and began speaking urgently to the person on the other end, Sarah felt herself shrinking inside. She sipped her coffee and looked around, unable to hear what Hayley was saying.

"People are just pouring off those buses," Hayley said, snapping the phone shut. She was talking about the crowds outside the windows.

"She's not just a friend, is she? I'll give odds she's not even married." The words popped out of her mouth.

"Who?" Hayley frowned as if she didn't understand.

"Kristina."

Hayley looked down at her coffee.

"I don't want to know," she said when it was the only thing she did want to know.

Hayley nodded and said, "Let's not talk about it now. Okay? Let's not ruin what we just began." She smiled. "I can't wait to see your mom."

***

Sarah's mom and Pat Thompson emerged from the crowds as if conjured out of wishful thinking when instead they'd managed to connect by using cell phones. Her mother wore a red Badger knit headband over her ears. Glistening gray strands were replacing the reddish-blond hair of her youth.

Hayley threw herself at her. "You look terrific, Kate."

Sarah watched them with a stab of jealousy, noting the use of her mom's first name instead of Mrs. S, which Hayley had called her mom as a kid. It was so obvious that Hayley felt an unusual attachment to her mother. Why had she never noticed it?

Pat looked on, smiling, her light brown hair curling out from under a Green Bay Packers knit cap. She extended her hand and introduced herself.

People flowed around them as if they were embedded in the concrete. Before long they were nudged into the mass of people and carried along with the crowd toward Capitol Square. Hayley walked backward, taking photos of Kate and Pat and Sarah. "I'm going to put you on the web. You have to look at my site— *hayleybites.com/blog*."

When she was done, Hayley turned around and linked arms with Sarah, tickling her ear with her breath. "You look just like your mom."

***

Late in the afternoon, Sarah sat across the aisle from her mom and Pat on one of the school buses that made up the shuttles. They were heading away from the Capitol toward East Towne Mall. Hayley had left for the airport. The past few days seemed surreal. She leaned back, closing her eyes in order to better picture Hayley saying goodbye.

She'd given Sarah's mom a big kiss and hug and then gave the same to Sarah, holding her for a long moment before whispering in her ear. "I've wanted to kiss your mom since I was a kid."

Sarah had pulled away and said firmly, "Goodbye, Hayley."

"I'll be in touch." She'd winked at Sarah and grinned at Kate. "Nice to meet you," she'd said to Pat.

"Fly safe," Sarah's mom had called.

Sarah sighed, dismayed at her feelings. Taken in again, she was appalled at the gaping hole yawning in front of her that Hayley's leaving had created. She knew by now that only she was in charge of her happiness. She had filled the emptiness with her work. By turning to the protests, she had found new meaning and friends and hope.

CHAPTER FOUR

Summer 1997

At breakfast the next morning, Sarah was sure her mom could smell sex on her. She smelled it on herself, although she'd scrubbed her hands. She had told Hayley they needed to get in the lake or take a shower, but Sarah's mom had breakfast waiting when they came downstairs in their swimsuits, still damp from the day before.

"We were just going for an early swim, Mom," she'd said, shivering in the morning air.

"Look at you. You're cold. Come sit down and eat first."

She glanced at Hayley for help, but Hayley only grinned. "I'm starving."

Her mom sat down next to her and passed the pancakes and bacon. "You okay, honey?" She rubbed her back. "You look tired."

She was tired and jumpy. What would her mom say if she knew? "I'm okay."

"You were thrashing around last night." Hayley's grin widened.

She shot a startled look at her friend and laughed. She couldn't help it. They'd both thrashed around and moaned as if in pain or ecstasy. It was a wonder her mom hadn't heard.

"The cicadas pretty much drowned everything out. So what are you two going to do today?"

The girls looked at each other. "Is there something you want us to do, Mrs. S?"

"You can start with cleaning up the breakfast dishes. I'm going to begin wading through the letter packet I brought with me."

Sarah dried, because she knew where everything went. When the phone rang, she answered.

"Hey, we need a spotter. You guys want to ski?" a male voice said.

"Mike?"

"Yeah. Is Hayley there?"

She handed Hayley the phone. She tucked it between her tan shoulder and chin.

"Yeah, sure. Whose boat? That jerk! No, I'll ski." She handed the phone back. "Fast Eddie's boat. He's always pawing me. You remember him, don't you? He's from Chicago." She leaned toward Sarah and gave her a kiss. "You can paw me anytime."

Sarah looked around for her mom. "You can't do that, Hayley."

"Why not? You taste so good."

"My mom…"

"What do you think she would do?" Hayley sent a few soapy bubbles her way.

She jumped back. "Hey," she said. "I don't want Mom to find out. Okay?" She tried hard to look serious but broke down laughing, imagining her mother's face.

"It wasn't that funny," Hayley said.

"Let me in on the joke," Sarah's mom said, coming into the kitchen.

Sarah squirted in her swimsuit and ran for the john.

At nine thirty, she and Hayley were sitting on the end of the pier, swishing their feet in the water, waiting for Fast Eddie and Mike. Sarah wore a T-shirt over her swimsuit. They had taken a little swim to wash off the scent of the night and were now drying out.

A Ski Nautique sped across the lake. The driver cut the power and rocked on the boat's wake just off Sarah's pier. Eddie Vandenberg was at the wheel. Mike leaned over and caught hold of a pier post and held on. Mike wore long swim trunks, barely hanging from his hips. A shock of hair the color of Hayley's fell over his forehead.

Eddie's grandparents owned a cottage on the other side of the lake. He sat behind the wheel, grinning at them with a crowded mouthful of white teeth. He'd always hung around with Mike, even though he was two years older. When he stood up, he grabbed his crotch, a habit Sarah remembered. She looked at Hayley, and they both rolled their eyes.

"Are they still there, Eddie?" Hayley asked.

"Just checking," he said, unabashed, tossing a shank of dishwater blond hair out of his eyes. "C'mon, get in."

Eddie grabbed at Hayley as she made her way toward the back of the boat. "Sit with me, you gorgeous broad."

She and Sarah sat down behind him on seats facing aft.

"Wanna go first?" Eddie asked Mike.

Mike shrugged into a life vest and jumped in, and Hayley handed him a slalom ski. She began feeding out line as Eddie started the engine and moved away from the pier.

"Hit it," Mike yelled.

Eddie pushed the lever forward, and Mike rose out of the lake on one ski. In a short time he was crossing the wake, his body leaning toward the waves. An arc of water sprayed out from under the ski.

"Wow!" Sarah said enviously.

"We'll have you doing that in no time," Eddie shouted.

"Can you do it?" she asked Hayley.

Hayley was holding her hair with one hand as she kept an eye on Mike. "All it takes is practice," she said.

Eddie reached behind the seat and opened a cooler. He extracted a can of beer and popped it open, then slugged some of it down. "Help yourself," he yelled.

Beer flowed down Sarah's throat, cooling her. She hoped it would give her courage.

When it was her turn, she tried to beg off. She'd seen Hayley circle the lake, perfectly balanced, her slender body curved toward the water, her long hair sometimes seeming to dip into the waves.

Hayley would have none of her protests. She helped Sarah into a life jacket, tightening the straps around her waist. "Come on, girl, show us your stuff."

The water closed around her as she pulled the boots over her feet. She would have to use two skis. Her major worry was embarrassing herself in front of the others.

Her mom waved from the shore, and Sarah lifted a hand. "Ready," she yelled and the boat took off, pulling her to her feet as if she weighed nothing. She rode the valley between the wakes until she felt brave enough to bob over one and parallel the craft.

Three times she tried to drop a ski when Eddie drove past her pier. Twice she took a nosedive into the water and somersaulted before popping through the surface. The third time she managed to wobble on one ski for what seemed a long time. When she hit the lake, water tunneled up her ass. She swam to the boat with the ski and climbed the ladder.

"Tomorrow you'll be a pro," Eddie said as she stepped into the boat.

She ran shaky hands over her hair as Hayley wrapped her in a towel.

"You got almost all the way around the lake on one ski," Hayley said, giving her a hug.

Eddie put on a life jacket and jumped into the water, and Hayley took over the controls. Sarah sat next to her. Mike grumbled about not driving as he took the spotter's seat behind Hayley.

"Hit it," Eddie yelled and barreled through the resisting lake before emerging on one ski in a rainbow of water.

***

That night Eddie joined them around the small fire on the public beach. He brought a small bag of marijuana and papers to roll it in. Sarah took puffs as one was passed around, even though it kind of gagged her. The stars spun overhead. The conversation, such as it was, slipped out of her consciousness and into the night.

She staggered with Hayley down the beach to her house around midnight. She felt an odd disassociation with her body. They tripped over bushes and over each other, falling twice, and laughed helplessly at their clumsiness, at nothing and everything.

When the screen slapped shut behind them, they said "Shhh" in unison and nearly fell down, hooting. Sarah's sides hurt and she was clutching them when her mom appeared at the foot of the stairs.

"Whew," her mom said without humor. "You stink of beer and dope."

Sarah drew herself up. She was eighteen, after all, old enough to vote. "We're not driving."

"Excellent logic," her mom snapped. "I'll see you in the morning."

They couldn't stop their hysterics, though. Dragging themselves up the stairs, breaking out into loud giggles and snorts, they reached Sarah's bed and threw themselves upon it.

Hayley's mom called the next morning while she and Sarah were choking down toast and gulping water. Sarah had already thrown up twice and thought she was about to do so again.

"Okay, Mom. I'll give him a call," Hayley said. "Yeah, I just took a few days off." She dropped the phone on the hook with a clang and made her way back to the table. "Mom found out I wasn't working. Looks like I'll have to go back." She plopped down and put her face in her hands. "God, I feel like shit."

Sarah longed to stick her head under water. It throbbed along with her heaving stomach.

"Do you think your mom is mad?" Hayley asked.

"Didn't she meet us at the stairs last night?" She remembered very little about the previous evening but was pretty sure that had happened.

"Maybe we woke her up. We were kind of crazy." Hayley's bloodshot eyes met Sarah's. "I'm sorry. I wanted to spend the summer with you."

After changing into their swimsuits, they slunk out the side door and down the steps to the beach, where they slipped around the boathouse, thus avoiding Sarah's mother who was reading on the beach. Her mother was the last person Sarah wanted to talk to, although she thought her mom caught sight of them before they disappeared into the bushes on the other side of the small building.

"I don't think she wants to see us either," Hayley said.

Sarah's head pounded with each step and vomit lurched up her throat. "I've got to sit down."

They placed their towels on the cool sand under a pine tree, and Sarah covered her face with her arms. "God, I think I'm going to die."

"Me too." Hayley lay on her belly, her arms under her cheek, her coppery hair bright where the sunlight reached it.

Sarah woke to the growl of Eddie's motor. She heard his voice and Mike's talking to her mom. When she sat up, the headache returned with a vengeance and she nearly spun out. She had no wish to ski. She thought she might blow apart if she hit the water.

Striped with shadows, Hayley slept on. Parched, Sarah snuck into the house and filled a couple of glasses with ice water after Eddie drove off.

"Hey, want some?" She nudged Hayley awake.

"God, yeah. My tongue is stuck to my mouth." She struggled to a sitting position and drank half of one glass. "Was that Eddie I heard?"

"Yep. I'm never going to drink and smoke at the same time again."

Hayley gave a throaty laugh. She wrapped her brown arms around her tan legs. "Hey, wanna?"

She did. She couldn't look at Hayley anymore and not think about the silky excitement of her. How had she put up with the clumsiness of Tim? Had she been as inept?

***

Hayley went home that night. She worked from seven till three at a gas station that sold everything from fuel to bait to tackle to ice cream. Sarah moped around the house the first part of the day. Her mother finally exploded midmorning.

"Do something. Clean your room, read a book, go for a swim, but don't sulk. You're lucky to be here."

She was insulted and blurted, "I know that, Mom."

"Do you know how dangerous it is to mix marijuana with beer? That stuff destroys brain tissue. Lots of people drown when they swim after using drugs."

"We weren't swimming," she said sullenly.

"Look, I don't want to worry about you doing something stupid when you're drunk out of your mind."

She was suddenly curious. "Didn't you ever get drunk, Mom?"

"Of course." She waved a hand in a helpless gesture and said lamely, "I was worried about you."

"I can take care of myself."

Her mother turned abruptly. Contrite, because she thought her mom was hiding tears, she touched her arm. She wanted to say she'd never drink and smoke again, but she knew she probably would. "I'm going down to the lake unless you need me."

Her mom turned and hugged her tightly. "Go. I'll be down soon."

She slipped away.

***

Eddie found her there in his Ski Nautique. His little brother, Joey, was with him. Mike wasn't. He sheared evergreens during the week, shaping them like cones. Once mostly fields and farms, their sandy county now bragged of being the Christmas tree capital of the world.

Sarah had just tumbled into the water to cool off. The hours had ticked off slowly. She emerged, treading water and shaking her head.

"Want to ski?" Eddie asked and waved at her mom on the shore.

She didn't, not really, but she knew she had to master one ski or lower her esteem in Hayley's eyes. "Okay. Hi, Joey."

Joey gave her the skis and by the time Hayley and Mike were back from work, standing on the pier, she had managed to find her balance. Eddie cut the engine and grabbed one of the pier posts. "She swallowed a ton of water, but she did it."

"We saw her. She looked great," Hayley said with a big grin. She had on her teeny bikini, and Eddie gawked at her as he had the day before.

"So do you," he said.

"Yeah, yeah." Hayley stepped into the boat and batted his hand away from her leg.

He reached into his cooler and brought out a beer. "Want one?"

"Yuck," Sarah said as Hayley slid into the backseat next to her. Mike sat up front next to Eddie.

"What do you want to do tonight? Roast around a fire or go to Indian Crossing? The Jamming Jets are playing. We could rock and roll." He stood up and gyrated in place, grabbing his crotch.

Sarah grasped her sides, nearly collapsing with laughter.

Also howling, Hayley winked at her. "What do you want to do?"

Sarah wanted to lie down somewhere with Hayley. It was what she thought about nearly all the time—the feel of Hayley—lips, skin, taut muscles, soft breasts. She understood Eddie's obsession with sex. She longed to run her hands all over Hayley, but those were feelings she had to hide. "Are you staying over?"

"If your mom's not tired of my sorry ass."

Eddie laughed. "You can stay at my place if she is."

"Mike can stay with you," Hayley suggested.

"Hey, no way. We got some girls coming to the fire tonight," Mike said.

Hayley took a swipe at her brother's head, but he ducked. He was bigger than she was now and no longer at her mercy. "Way to go! We don't want to horn in on your party. You driving to Indian Crossing, Eddie?"

***

Hayley went home to get dressed. Her mom had been complaining that she never saw her anymore.

In the small kitchen Sarah wiped one bare foot against her leg and then the other. "I have to shower, Mom. We're going out tonight. When's dinner?"

"Whenever you fix it. I'm eating right now." The thin smile told Sarah her mother was pissed.

"What are you fixing?"

"Tuna fish salad. There's a little left over. There's some cantaloupe too."

"Don't you like Hayley anymore?"

Her mother turned and looked her straight in the eyes. "Of course I like Hayley. I don't much like what you're doing with your time, but I don't blame her for that."

"Mom, that was one night."

"I don't suppose you're going to be driving around drinking tonight, are you?" she said sarcastically. "What does Eddie carry around in that cooler?"

"That doesn't mean I'm drinking any of it."

"You're driving with Eddie when he's impaired."

Sarah laughed. "He's always been impaired, Mom."

Her mother grinned, and Sarah felt relief. "I'll eat tuna on toast if there is enough."

Eddie drove a 1986 Ford Escort wagon that had belonged to his dad. It ticked loudly. Rust licked at the doors. A chunk fell off when Sarah slammed hers.

"We lose some of the car every time someone gets in." He laughed. On the floor of the front seat she saw a cooler. Sure enough, he pulled a beer can out and hung it over the backseat. "You girls going to sit in the back and make me feel like a taxi driver?"

"Isn't anyone else going?" Hayley asked. Her hair was kinky from the humidity. It clung to her cheeks. "No beer, not right now."

Sarah pushed her own heavy hair away from her face and unrolled the window. She smelled the beer as Eddie popped the tab. "No thanks."

"Mark Sorenson. You remember him, don't you?"

"What's he gonna do now that he's graduated?"

"Going into agriculture. His dad owns the biggest vegetable farm around."

They picked Mark up on County Highway K. The house and barns were impressive compared to those in the rest of the county. Two huge John Deere tractors were parked in the driveway as if someone had just jumped off and gone inside.

A quiet guy, Mark guffawed once in a while at Eddie's jokes, but mostly he stared out the window. Eddie and Mark slugged back beers as they drove to the dance hall.

They'd left at near dark. In her youth, Sarah's mom had told her about the bigger, better-known bands that had once played at Indian Crossing. The large white-painted wood building with the open wooden shutters stood in the middle of a parking lot near the Chain of Lakes. Nightlife began around nine thirty.

The Escort's door creaked with resistance as Sarah pushed it open. She walked down to a lake with Hayley and kicked off her shoes. The night was hot, and she stepped into the wavelets lapping the shore. A streak of red zigzagged among purplish clouds along the dark horizon across the water. A thin moon floated in a hazy cloud. The damp air clung to her hair and skin.

Along the shore, milkweed gave off a strong, sweet smell. God, she loved summer—smelly and hot and humid, just like this. Hayley's hand tapped hers as they walked down the short beach to the first cottage. They linked little fingers.

More cars pulled into the parking lot. Mark and Eddie were standing with a group of guys, talking and laughing loudly. She heard the band warming up. She wasn't much of a dancer, probably because she didn't really like to put herself out there for others to watch.

When the dancing began, the guys gathered around the walls, sitting on the sills of the propped up wood openings. Smoke drifted toward the dim overhead lights. The smell of beer filled the hall. The Jamming Jets started with old songs like "Smoke Gets in Your Eyes." Eddie grabbed Hayley's hand and hauled her out on the dance floor where no one else had dared to venture. He swung her around like she was a manikin. Her feet occasionally left the floor. She was laughing and slapping at his hands.

"What? What? Don't you like to dance?" he asked when the song was over.

"That's not dancing. I felt like a rag doll."

The band started "Boogie Woogie Blues," and Eddie grabbed his crotch first and Hayley's hand second. He dragged her back to the dance floor, where girls were now dancing together, and threw her around in a wild rendition of a jitterbug.

Helplessly bent over, Sarah and Mark shouted with laughter, but when she asked if he wanted to dance, he went pale with terror. Most boys did not jitterbug. Actually, most girls didn't either anymore, but Sarah's dad had taught her and her sister to dance when they were little. He would snatch them up and lead them around the room in a fox-trot or a jitterbug. He still did.

"I'm going outside," he said abruptly. "Want to come?"

She didn't want to be left alone like a wallflower, so she tripped down the steps after him. He pulled a pack of cigarettes out of his pocket and held it out to her. She took one, although she wasn't a smoker. He lit hers. His profile flashed in the light—thin-lipped, narrow-eyed with pale brown hair.

"Want to walk?" he asked.

The cigarette not only made her lightheaded, but it shut out the smells of the night. She felt sort of out of control, open to whatever he suggested. His hand closed over hers as they strolled toward Eddie's Escort. She dropped her half-smoked cigarette on the gravel.

Mark opened the back door and pushed her inside. He shoved in after her, tossing his burning butt out the still-open door. They were parked near the weedy edge of the parking lot away from the lights.

He breathed smoke into her with a kiss, and his tongue snaked into her mouth—thick and wet. In a few seconds he was groping her breasts. Before she could pull away, his hand slithered down to her crotch.

Whenever anyone touched her there, she got wet. She thought she must be the horniest person alive. She could come in a matter of minutes, but Mark's touch was a little too rough. It gave her the opportunity to attempt to break away.

His muscles bulged under his T-shirt as he forced her down on the backseat and fumbled with his zipper. She felt his prick, hot and urgent against her belly.

"No," she said in panic.

"I've got a rubber," he said.

"Let's just talk. Okay?"

"About what?" He loosened his grip.

"Anything. Eddie and Hayley will be looking for us."

"Nah."

The door opened, and Hayley said, "Hey, what's going on here?"

Sarah jumped out the other door and stood panting in the weeds, her heart pounding. "Nothing."

"What happened out there in the car with Mark?" Hayley asked later in the dark of Sarah's bedroom.

"He tried to rape me."

"I want to rape you," Hayley growled, and Sarah forgot all about Mark as they tussled on the bed.

CHAPTER FIVE

Winter 2011

The protests moved with the governor. One was held outside the Radisson in downtown Appleton one night, where a Republican Party meeting was scheduled. The weather had turned cold and snow was falling. Sarah and Jane and Margaret took signs and waded through several inches of slush, which seeped into Sarah's shoes. A bitter wind tunneled down College Avenue. Once again she was freezing.

When she went home to her one-bedroom apartment to take a hot shower, disappointed that there were no messages on her voice mail, she poured herself a vodka and tonic as sort of a consolation prize and took it to the bathroom.

The phone rang, and she bolted out of the shower, slipping on the bathroom floor and banging her hip on the cabinets. She grabbed the receiver on the third ring. "Hello," she said, dripping water on the tile floor.

"You sound breathless," Hayley said, amusement in her voice.

"I just came home from another protest."

"In Madison?"

"No. There was a Republican dinner here. The governor was supposed to come. If he came, we never saw him. It was cold and snowy. What's happening with you?"

"Just working on my blog. Have you looked at it?"

"Of course. You're very clever. I liked what you wrote about last weekend." Actually, Sarah thought Hayley could have written more about her impressions and less about the facts.

"Thanks. So, what are you doing?"

"Warming up in the shower."

"I'm coming on Friday. I have the same room reserved."

She carried the phone into the bathroom and wrapped herself in a towel. "I work Friday till four."

"Meet me at the Madison airport at seven fifteen on Friday. We'll drive to the hotel together. You have a car, don't you?"

She did, of course—an older Focus wagon with seventy-five thousand miles on it. She had been waiting to hear Hayley's plans so that she could become part of them and was too excited to be dismayed by the strange things her heart was doing. Like the kid she'd been, she let herself be drawn toward the elusive prize— Hayley.

Hayley lowered her voice. Someone was talking in the background. "I'll call tomorrow."

"There's a meeting tomorrow night." There were always meetings. Planning meetings, organizational meetings. There were also phone banks. She had one of those Wednesday evening. She sometimes wondered what was more important—doing her job or making sure she had one.

"I have to go. See you soon."

She took a swig of her watered-down drink and hopped back in the shower. It had been a woman's voice in the background. Probably Kristina. Maybe she could lure Hayley back home, at least part time, she thought before scoffing at herself. Hayley had made it amply clear that her home was New York City. She rinsed off and got out.

She hadn't realized how lonely she was till last weekend and not just for anyone. She had gone to gay bars, to lesbian potlucks, to gay political groups and to parties after she broke up with James. She'd trailed Molly home after a lesbian outing. They'd had enthusiastic but not very good sex and a month later considered themselves a couple. Sarah had liked Molly very much, but she hadn't loved her. She'd realized that quickly. However, it was easier to stay than to go. It had been fun having someone to come home to and do things with. She'd really go for that again, but with Hayley.

***

Friday seemed like a forever day. She had packed and loaded the car Thursday evening. She'd received e-mail from Hayley that evening, a reminder of her expected time of arrival—as if Sarah could possibly forget.

She threw her briefcase on the passenger side, slid into the cold seat and wheeled out of the parking lot. The roads were buffeted by high winds. Snow swirled toward her windshield. Daylight went quickly, and a steady stream of headlights filled her windshield and rearview mirror. There was no good way to get to Madison from where she lived. She had to drive two sides of a triangle—US Highway 41 south to State Road 23 west.

Nothing could tame the excitement building in her, though. She had to force herself to concentrate on driving and hope the weather hadn't affected Hayley's flight. When she reached the Madison airport, she parked and ran inside, chased by the wind. She bought a cup of stale decaf and sat down to wait.

Sarah never went anywhere without a book. It was one of the things her mother had drilled into her. Halfway through *The Girl Who Played with Fire*, which she'd hardly been able to put down, she found her gaze straying to the landing strip. She missed seeing the plane land, though, and looked up in time for her breath to catch in her throat as a flush suffused her.

Hayley's backpack was thrown over her shoulder, her computer case in her other hand. She wore jeans and a Columbia jacket and was talking on her cell phone, which she snapped shut and pocketed before she reached Sarah.

Sarah stood up, fumbling with her keys and book, and Hayley kissed her smack on the mouth. She fell back on the bench. "Can't you wait till we're alone?" she asked.

"Nope. I'm just that glad to see you." She was grinning.

"Me too." Too glad, she thought. Hayley was filling up all the spaces in her life.

They walked out into the icy wind and ran through spitting snow to Sarah's car. Even with her down jacket, her mittens and scarf, Sarah felt the bite. She hadn't put on the knit cap that would flatten her hair. In fact, this time she'd brought earmuffs instead.

"It's goddamn cold out," Hayley said.

"Big change in temps from last week." They grinned at each other across the front seat, and Sarah's heart beat out of sync. She took a deep breath and told herself to calm down.

"What's going on tonight?" Hayley asked as Sarah drove out of the airport and headed toward downtown.

"They're still camped out in the Capitol."

"I know. I've been watching MSNBC. Wisconsin is Egypt in America right now, but it doesn't seem to faze your governor."

She sighed. "I know. He says we're all outside agitators, if that isn't ridiculous."

"Think the Democratic senators are coming back any time soon?"

"I hope not."

Hayley threw an arm across Sarah's seat and began playing with her hair. "Miss me?"

She hadn't been able to think about Hayley and get anything done. She'd dreamed through meetings, jerked back to reality by someone's unexpected question. She'd even forgotten her spiel when she was phone banking. "You could say so."

Hayley withdrew her hand, and with it went the goose bumps. "Me too. New York is a long way from here in lots of ways." She looked out the window. People were converging on the Capitol. She guided Sarah to the hotel's parking garage.

After checking in, they carried their backpacks to the room. Hayley dumped hers inside the door and turned to Sarah.

"You smell delicious," she said into Sarah's hair. "You know you have your own special odor." She lifted Sarah's chin and kissed her—slowly this time. "How about a quickie?"

"Hayley, who is Kristina?" She hadn't meant to say this, to spoil things from the get-go.

Hayley swung away in apparent frustration. "Sometimes, Sweeney, you have to just let things work themselves out."

"I can't…"

"And I can't afford to live alone in New York. Isn't our hooking up again something of a miracle? Wasn't last weekend special?"

"Yes, but…" She met Hayley's green eyes and looked away.

"Can we just not talk about Kristina? Let's go get something to eat."

What right did she have to question Hayley anyway? "Okay." And they went out into the freezing night.

The streets were crowded, the restaurants full. They finally found a place to sit down around nine and got back to the hotel close to eleven. As usual, Sarah had been up since before six. One beer had slowed her down. Two had nearly put her under.

In the mirror she looked hollow-eyed at Hayley peering over her shoulder. Hayley pulled the elastic tie out of her hair and shook it out.

Sarah turned on a whim and brushed its thickness off Hayley's shoulders. "You have great hair."

Hayley's hands closed over her upper arms. "Thanks." She kissed Sarah. "This is beginning to seem like home." Her hands rounded Sarah's back and pulled her close. She sighed.

"Why the sigh?" Sarah mumbled into Hayley's hair. To her sighs usually meant something was wrong.

"I'm just so content."

Sarah was more than content. She was ecstatic, stretched tight with expectation. Her skin tingled. Bed was just around the corner.

Under the covers, they held each other for what seemed a long time and Hayley muttered about her long week. Neither made a move. Hayley's breathing lengthened and she let out a snort that made them both jump. Sarah felt a keen disappointment, and then sleep overtook her too.

She woke up looking into the shadows of Hayley's face, framed by a curtain of hair. A painful jolt of excitement zipped through her. Hayley's hand was already between her legs. She laced fingers in Hayley's hair and tasted her lips, warm and swollen with sleep. Hayley pushed her T-shirt up and nuzzled her breasts, and they both wriggled out of their tops and panties.

Their bodies met at the same places, and they strained toward each other with hands and mouths and hips. The moment of climax came quickly, causing them to pause and gasp and slowly collapse against each other.

When they fell apart, Sarah brushed her wet mouth with the back of her hand and turned her head toward Hayley. Despite an uncertain shyness, she had to see Hayley's expression, to know if she had experienced the same intensity.

Hayley's voice was hoarse. "Well, Sweeney, that should have made you hungry. It did me. Should we see what's going on outside?" A streak of daylight leached between the heavy drapes.

The words left Sarah feeling flat. Had she felt a connection that had escaped Hayley? "Sure." She rolled out of bed and into the shower.

But then Hayley climbed into the tub with her, and they took turns washing each other's hair and bodies.

***

They sat in the windowsill at the coffee shop on King Street. The tables were taken. They'd used up a big bite of the morning by staying in bed late, and the line leading to the union members who were grilling and giving away brats and free pop had been deep and long when they passed Wisconsin Avenue. The school buses shuttling people from the malls were unloading. Blue Bird buses, also run by the unions, were depositing demonstrators from cities around the state.

Sarah had never seen so many people at one time. Her heart swelled with pride. Margaret Dempson had been right. The governor had awakened more than the unions, though. His attempts to force his agenda down the electorate's throat were being met with a fierce resistance. On this cold and snowy day, better spent inside, protesters were out in force.

On Thursday, the governor had been fooled by a bogus call from a liberal online newspaperman, pretending to be one of the billionaires who had helped finance his campaign—David Koch. The conversation had been taped and sent to the media. Walker admitted to thinking about bringing in outside agitators to stir things up. He laughed when it was suggested he take a baseball bat to negotiations. And he accepted an invitation to visit the Koch brothers in Cali when this was over. He thought the demonstrations would die down when the media stopped covering them.

"Amazing," Hayley said with a smile.

"Isn't it?" Sarah felt cold radiating through the glass.

"You are."

"Yeah, sure," she said modestly, hoping it wasn't Hayley's charm talking.

Outside, they joined the sea of people. Snow fell. The wind rushed at them on the corners. Firemen marched by, playing bagpipes, their hairy legs red with cold. The streets, the sidewalks, the terrace around the Capitol and the inside of the building itself held a crush of protesters.

The fourteen Democratic senators were still in Illinois, attempting to negotiate support among Republicans for retaining collective bargaining rights for public workers. Instead, their paychecks were being held hostage and their aides being harassed.

Someone with a megaphone shouted, "What does democracy look like?" and the passing crowd again roared, "This is what democracy looks like."

They grabbed a free sandwich around noon from a table outside a church and took it inside the Capitol. Hayley had been taking photos, occasionally stopping to interview someone. She asked a couple if they thought the demonstrations would change the governor's agenda.

"No, but maybe they'll change a few Republican senators' minds and if they don't, we'll recall them."

"Is there talk of a recall?"

"Sure. If you think the Budget Repair Bill is bad, wait till the budget comes out. The only way to stop them is to take back the state senate."

Sarah was listening. She knew the protests would end, but the thought of a future without them sent her into a small panic. Would Hayley return on weekends?

The long, cold day enervated her. By three she longed to sit down with Hayley in a warm place. She was chilled all the way through. Hayley put an arm around her and steered her toward the hotel.

***

She dropped Hayley off at the airport early Sunday afternoon and drove home. Reality set in as snow shot across the road in front of her. She sensed Hayley was torn between New York and Kristina and what was going on in Wisconsin and her. No matter how she tried she couldn't place Hayley in her life. Hayley loomed large in Sarah's mind—too big for her small apartment, her friends, even the Fox Cities.

Safely home, she booted up her computer. There was a protest at Green Bay late that afternoon. A Republican fund-raiser was planned on the south side. The governor was scheduled as speaker. Carpoolers were meeting at five. Jane e-mailed that she and Margaret would meet her at the designated carpool spot.

There was a chatty message from her mom who wrote that she would have gone to Saturday's protest, but she had a cold. Pat had gone with an old friend from Oshkosh. Had she seen her there?

She wrote back that no, she hadn't seen Pat among the thousands of protesters and added, "It was cold in Madison. I'm glad you stayed home. Miss you."

Winter Sundays were usually long for her. The protests and Hayley had changed that, at least for now. Sarah's friends were in relationships or marriages. Society seemed to go in twos. Her brother, who lived in Florida, was between women. Her sister was married with a baby girl whom they all adored. She saw them on holidays or during summer vacations at the lake. She wondered if at family gatherings Pat felt as if she were on the outside looking in.

When she pulled into the Shopko Express parking lot on Ballard and Highway 41, around fifteen cars were waiting. Jane and Margaret got out of one of them, zipping up jackets and pulling on hoods. Margaret said, "I'm getting tired of being out in the cold. Did you know it was estimated there were upward of seventy thousand people protesting in Madison yesterday?"

At least a thousand demonstrators had gathered at the cross street that led to the restaurant where the governor was to speak. They peered over shoulders to see what was going on as protesters milled around, waving signs and chanting. Police stood at the intersection behind roadblocks. When a black SUV drove slowly past, the crowd shouted, "Shame, shame."

At seven thirty, when the governor still hadn't arrived and Margaret was visibly shivering, Sarah said, "Want to go? There are enough people. No one will ever notice our absence." She was shaking with cold too.

When she was alone in the dark car heading toward home with the heater blasting, she checked her cell for voice mail. She'd felt the vibrations but hadn't answered, not wanting to talk to Hayley when the others were there.

"Back safely. See you next Friday. Let me know if they evict those camping in the Capitol building, will you?" The capital police had planned to do that on Saturday, but they hadn't wanted to use force against the so far peaceful protesters.

She longed to return the call, but often Hayley seemed distant when she did. She guessed Kristina was around, and it hurt.

CHAPTER SIX

1997 to 1998

The rest of the family arrived on a Friday in early August. Sarah spied Jeff, standing on the pier, waving both arms, as Fast Eddie's Ski Nautique rocketed around the end of the lake. The disappointment she felt was physical. She'd been dreading their coming. Hayley would no longer spend nights with her, and even if she did, there was no way they would be able to do it.

Doing it had become enormously important to Sarah. She was both ashamed of her neediness, because that's how she saw it, and terrified she and Hayley would be caught in the act. Her mom and dad would think she was a pervert, which was true. Jeff, who was always flipping a wrist when he thought some guy was gay, would be merciless.

Doing it was what she thought about when Hayley was at work. She walked around in a daze. Aware that her mother's questioning eyes followed her, she made attempts to at least look like she was reading a book when they were on the beach together.

Invariably, Eddie came to her rescue. He and his little brother and she would ski or speed around the shore's perimeter, showing off, passing time till Hayley and Mike got off work. Now Eddie pulled back on the throttle and the boat stopped, just like that. Its wake pushed it toward the pier.

"Cool, man," Jeff said over the idling motor as he jumped into the craft and slapped Eddie's hand. Eddie stood up and adjusted his crotch, and they both laughed. "Hey, Joey," Jeff called to Eddie's little brother. To Sarah, he said, "Hi, sis, what's happening?"

Beth ran out on the pier, her towel flying behind her. Sarah's sister didn't look like anyone in the family. Jeff was the spitting image of their dad. Sarah resembled her mom. Beth was tall and blond and built like Sarah wanted to be. She'd always thought maybe she'd grow into Beth, but now that she was eighteen, she knew that wasn't going to happen. Beth had always been the prettier daughter, the one who got most of the compliments. Like an afterthought, Sarah had to settle for cute.

She waved at her dad, who was standing on the beach with her mom. He raised a hand, then put an arm around her mother and they walked up to the house. She wondered if they were going to do it. When she first realized that her parents had done it more than three times—the necessary amount to have three kids—she had become curious about how often they did it. At first, it had grossed her out and then had intrigued her. Now that she was doing it, it had become an obsession.

Rather than ply her mother with questions all those years ago, she had asked Beth. "Do you think they take their clothes off?" She'd been trying to get a clear picture in her mind of her dad's hairy chest pressed to her mother's fair skin.

"I suppose," Beth had said and giggled.

Back then she hadn't been sure exactly how the act was accomplished. Why the penis became engorged with blood and why that would feel good. She'd thought it would hurt.

"Haven't you ever touched yourself down there?" Beth had asked.

It hadn't been something she'd wanted to admit to. She'd thought Beth might use it against her when she was mad at her. So she'd just looked at her blankly.

"Well, try it sometime."

"You do that?"

Beth had said in a snotty tone, "It's none of your business what I do," which was a dead giveaway that she did do it.

In the night she had squeezed her eyes shut and slid her fingers between her legs. She'd been doing it ever since, but it paled in comparison to doing it with Hayley.

She watched her sister take Eddie's hand and jump lithely into the boat. Sarah had ignored his hand and fallen over his big feet when she'd jumped in. Beth was a guy's girl, one who wouldn't even try to grab a snake or a crawdad behind the head. Once she'd been a great frog and turtle catcher, when they still had a lot of frogs hanging around and as long as the turtles were red-eared ones and not too big. Sarah still slammed on the brakes and jumped out to help a turtle cross the road before it got run over.

There were five of them in the boat when Eddie took off, pinning everyone to the seats. He loved to turn on the power when it was least expected. He would laugh and laugh when someone lost his or her balance.

"Go, Eddie," Jeff said, laughing with him.

"Where's Hayley?" Beth yelled into Sarah's ear.

"At work. She'll be home by four."

"Yeah? Mom said she's been living at the house."

Sarah's hair whipped around her face, catching in her mouth and eyes. "Is that a problem?"

"No, as long as she sleeps in your bed." She grinned, showing her white, straight teeth, and gave Sarah a friendly nudge.

Sarah hid a smile, thinking how crowded the bed was. They always locked the door and sometimes slept on an open sleeping bag on the floor.

"I can't wait to see her," Beth hollered over the engine noise.

The sun shone down through a thin sliver of clouds, deceptively cool. Eddie drove toward the center of the lake, opened his cooler and handed out beer. Jeff grabbed one, took a gulp and let out a loud belch.

"Good stuff," he said, rubbing his belly. He was long and thin with a dark shock of hair.

When they spied Hayley and Mike standing on the raft at the public beach, Eddie careened toward them. Both the raft and boat rocked, and Jeff stood up to help Hayley get in. He was staring, Sarah noticed. Hayley still hadn't bought another swimsuit. The bra barely covered her dark nipples.

"You look great, Hayley," he said with enthusiasm.

She gave him a crooked smile, almost like she enjoyed the attention. "Just don't touch," she said.

Beth was also looking, a question in her eyes. She lifted her brows.

"Haven't had time to shop," Hayley said.

"Who's on first?" Eddie asked. "You and Mike can ski together."

***

That night they all sat around the fire on the public beach. Eddie's cooler was anchored in the lake. He had brought a stash of marijuana. He rolled a joint and passed the burning cigarette around. The smell filled Sarah's nostrils.

No more sounds of frogs. Along with the lightning bugs, their reproductive cycles had come and gone. Fires dotted the shoreline. Voices echoed over the water, sometimes clearly understandable. A layer of clouds had settled along the western horizon and a pale streak of earlier purples and reds separated sky from trees.

Hayley was sitting between Sarah and Beth, her arms wrapped around her legs. Beth reached over and ran a hand down Hayley's bare skin. "You are always so brown."

Hayley laid her head on her knees. "I should have had you buy me a new swimsuit at the mall where you worked."

"I've got one that I bet will fit you."

"Cool."

"I hear you got a full boat to Brown." Beth took the homemade cigarette from Eddie, who was practically fastened to her side. Her face lit up in a flare from the fire.

Hayley lowered her voice. "Yeah. I lucked out." Brown was a topic Sarah and Hayley still avoided.

Sarah burned with jealousy. In less than two weeks they would return home and she'd leave for UW-Madison. She wondered how she would bear ten months without Hayley. She was unwilling to share her with Beth or Eddie or anyone else right now.

After sucking weed, she lay back on the sand, her arms under her head. The stars amidst their shreds of clouds spun. She closed her eyes and felt Hayley's hand flatten and creep under her hip. The possessive touch reassured her, even as she covered her face with an arm to hide tears.

She and Beth stumbled home around midnight, tripping through bushes. Hayley had left for her own place. Despite the heavy weight in her chest, Sarah laughed along with Beth whenever they bumped into something. Beth dropped a tennis shoe in the living room, and they paused in exaggerated caution. Snorts of suppressed laughter escaped them despite their best efforts, and they fell up the stairs and onto their beds, hooting one minute and sound asleep the next.

The two weeks flew by. A few times Hayley and Sarah managed to escape from the others and find a warm spot in the sand, where they groped each other. Satisfaction was quick but not lasting. No longer were there hours alone to talk and make love. That's how Sarah thought of doing it with Hayley, as making love. She was sure she would never love anyone else like she did Hayley.

"I'm going to miss you," she said on their last night together. She couldn't put into words how much.

"I'm going to miss this." Hayley looked solemn. She ran long fingers through Sarah's hair and leaned forward to kiss her. They were hiding in a small grove of white pines, lying on soft needles. The water lapped at the shore less than fifty feet away.

Sarah had only pretended to smoke and drink at the beach party that ended around one. She was dead sober and fighting the urge to bawl. The summer had been a watershed for her.

She could only move on, scared of losing Hayley. Only one fire burned across the lake. The night was quiet except for a whippoorwill calling repetitively. Another answered.

"Come on, let's take these off," Hayley urged, tugging on Sarah's T-shirt. "I want skin on skin."

They came together, their flesh still sun-warm, Hayley on top. Sarah flipped her on her back, and tears began sliding down her cheeks.

"Hey," Hayley whispered. "We'll talk, we'll write, and there'll always be next summer and the one after that and after that."

She grabbed her shorts off the sand and wiped her nose. She didn't think she could bear to watch the summer end.

"Hey, hey, hey," Hayley said even softer. "Come on. It's our last night. Let's stay here till the sun comes up. We'll do it till we can't anymore."

She took a deep, ragged breath to regain control. Hayley was nibbling on her neck, and she bent and did the same. Grains of sand crunched between her teeth. She tasted salt and smelled coconut oil. Unable to wait, she slid her hand into the tangle of hair between Hayley's legs. She loved to make her gasp.

***

The sun filtered through the taller pines behind them, turning the sky a pale blue and the few clouds a bright pink. A slight breeze rippled across the lake and stirred up the rosy hue the sun had laid down.

Sarah sat up in a daze. The sand was cool under her. It seemed like she'd just closed her eyes, which was pretty much true. It had been after four before they'd drifted off in an embrace. Her lips were sore. She touched them to see if they felt swollen. She tingled between her legs, where it was sticky and a little tender.

Had anyone looked for them last night? She would have heard their calls and seen their flashlights. Everyone else had been pretty doped up, including Beth. They were probably all still asleep.

She thought of her bags, packed and sitting on the floor in her room. It made her immeasurably sad, and she was wiping away tears again when Hayley opened her pale green eyes. "You gotta stop that," she said in a hoarse voice. "Think anyone will see us if we jump in the lake? We reek of sex."

Sarah glanced at her watch. It was not quite six. Cedar waxwings keened from a dead oak near the lake. She fell on Hayley, making her snort a laugh. Afterward, they waded into the sandy lake in their underwear. The water closed around Sarah like a cool caress, and she shivered. Some guys in a fishing boat were watching them, but she didn't care. A bra and panties covered her as much as her swimsuit did.

When the bottom dropped out from under them, Hayley pulled her under and kissed her. They broke through the surface, desperate for air. The blood in Sarah's veins felt like water.

"I'm going to miss you something fierce, Sarah Sweeney," Hayley said.

Of course, that made Sarah cry again. She washed the tears away, knowing her face was puffy. Her mom would notice. So would Beth.

They covered their wet underwear with their shorts and T-shirts and walked barefoot to Sarah's house. Sarah's toes dragged in the sand. A fist tightened in her chest, and she thought this must be what heartbreak felt like.

Hayley followed her into the house to say goodbye. The door slapped shut behind them, and they paused to listen to the voices in the kitchen.

When they appeared in the doorway, Sarah's mom looked them over. "Where have you been?"

"Swimming," Hayley said.

Beth's eyebrows lifted in question. She had to know Sarah hadn't come home last night.

"Come on and eat," Sarah's dad said. "You too, Hayley."

They sat side by side and Hayley wolfed down bacon and scrambled eggs, while Sarah struggled to force food down her throat. The passage seemed to have closed. Whenever she looked up, she saw her mom's concerned gaze on her.

Hayley hugged everyone before she left. Sarah wanted to walk her home, but Sarah's dad said there wasn't time. They stood outside together for a few minutes.

"Hey, before we know it we'll be back here," Hayley said. "God, I'm going to miss you, though."

Sarah's breath caught as she struggled not to cry. She forced out, "Me too."

They hugged goodbye. "I love you, Sweeney," Hayley said in her ear.

"I love you, Baxter." Sarah's voice broke on "Baxter."

She stood for a moment, watching Hayley walk away. When she turned back to the house, she nearly bumped into her mother.

Her mom said, "I don't know where you were last night and I know we've talked about this before, but if you're going to fool around, you need to carry condoms."

She stared at her mom as heat flashed through her. She knew what an effort it must have taken for her mom to say what she had.

"I know, Mom." She would have laughed, but she thought she might never laugh again. "I have to get my stuff."

***

Sarah slept most of the way home. She rode in the backseat of her dad's Taurus while Beth sat up front. Jeff and her mom followed. Her mom had promised Jeff that he could drive and the car was a small one. In three and a half hours they were unloading in the middle of a heat wave. There was no lake with a breeze, only a shallow pond with a waterspout in the middle of the subdivision where they lived. The bottom of it was covered with duck shit. Not even kids were allowed to wade in it. However, there was a swimming pool at the clubhouse, which Sarah used on occasion. They had been spoiled by chlorine-free water, by their own sandy beach, and as soon as she finished her education, she planned to seek a job close to the lake.

Now that she was home, though, she was ready to move to Madison. She'd been assigned a roommate, whose letter was waiting for her among the pile of mail. Her name was Brook Esterberger. Sarah tore open the envelope.

"I am so excited about going to UW-Madison. Can't wait to meet you," it read and went on with a few details about her life.

"It's pretty boring here right now. I'm packing everything I own. How about you?"

Sarah studied the picture of a girl with a beautiful smile and tried not to hate her for taking Hayley's place.

Her mom looked over her shoulder and uncannily spoke as if she was reading Sarah's mind. "I know she's not Hayley, but she looks nice enough. Give her a chance, Sarah. Maybe she had someone else she wanted for a roommate too." She put a hand on Sarah's shoulder before walking away.

***

Brook was tossing clothes in drawers when Sarah and her mom and dad crowded into the small room with Sarah's stuff. She wasn't as pretty as the picture, which had been professionally touched up. She was shorter than Sarah and heavier, with one eyebrow that seemed to be permanently notched with irony.

She gestured at a box fan in the window. "Don't know if that's doing anything but stirring up the heat, but hey, I think I'd be a puddle without it."

"I think a fan is just what you need," Sarah's mom said.

"Yeah, thanks for bringing one," Sarah added.

"You can have this bed if you want," Brook said to Sarah. "I don't really care, or we could move the furniture."

Two bunk beds, both uppers, were crammed on either side of the window. A desk was slid under each with a dresser pushed against the wall at the end of both beds. Two closets were on either side of the door. This left little room for extras like Sarah's tiny microwave and Brook's small TV. Brook had also brought a futon so that they would have something else to sit on besides the beds or desk chairs.

"Looks good to me," Sarah said.

"I'm going to get some boxes. I don't know where we're going to put all this stuff," Sarah's dad said, disappearing out the door.

"We'll find a place," her mom called.

"Be right back," Sarah said, following them.

When her parents left, she and Brook walked to Memorial

Union and sat on the terrace next to Lake Mendota. Students milled around them. They strolled to the far end of the pier, and Sarah tried not to think of Hayley and the ache she had created just by leaving. She wondered again how she'd get through the long winter.

However, she hadn't bargained for the excitement of living in Madison, the challenge of her classes, her part-time job answering phones at the front desk, her friendship with Brook. These would make the year fly by.

She wrote to Hayley at the end of every day and spent too many of her waking hours reliving the summer. In bed at night she pretended Hayley lay next to her. She masturbated quietly under the covers—so much that she sometimes worried about offending the god she claimed not to believe in.

***

When the university let out in May, she asked her mom and dad if she could find a job near the lake and stay there for the summer.

Her dad said, "We could use you at work this summer."

Her hopes plummeted. She had written to Mr. Jenkins at the gas station and sports shop where Hayley had worked the previous summer. She'd also asked Hayley to put in a word for her. Her hope was that she and Hayley could live together at Sarah's house on the lake, at least until Sarah's family showed up for vacation. She thought she would die if her parents kept her home even part of the summer.

"What are you going to drive?" her dad asked.

"I thought maybe Mom could take me there and I could hitch rides with Hayley." Hayley was allowed to use an old truck to drive to work.

Her mom was watching her closely. "I could take her and spend a week or two in June and then go back in July for the rest of the summer."

Her heart raced with hope. In her mind she was already on her way.

"Wouldn't you like to invite Brook up for a week or two?"

Yes, of course, she would, but that would mean no sex with

Hayley, and she didn't think she could stand that. She frowned and said, "I'll be working" as if she already had a job.

Beth had a job at the same shop at the mall. Jeff worked part-time for a construction company and played baseball. Sarah cared only about being with Hayley and would even shear Christmas trees with Mike to be at the lake.

***

She and her mom were talking majors on the drive north. Sarah hadn't settled on a major but knew she'd end up teaching something. It might as well be something she was good at, like English lit and/or composition and grammar. She glanced at the dash. She was driving, going seventy-five miles an hour, her entire being pulling her toward Hayley.

Her mom leaned over and looked too. "What's the all-fired rush?"

"What did you want to do, Mom?" She eased up on the accelerator with difficulty. It was always harder to slow down and once again the speedometer began to creep up.

"To be a writer or an editor, something to do with books, but then I married your dad and Beth came along."

She threw a glance at her mother and caught her ironic smile. "You are a writer. You write an advice column."

"A writer of few words, inspired by others."

"I think you're good at what you do. You help people." She was feeling magnanimous now that she was on her way to the lake.

Hayley wasn't home, of course. After unloading and helping her mom put groceries away, Sarah called Jenkins Gas and Sports Center. Hayley answered.

"Hey, are you at the lake? At last?"

Sarah smiled. "Yeah, we just got here. Is your boss around?"

"I'll get him. He said maybe he'll be able to use you in July when summer really kicks in."

Her heart, which had jumped joyously at the sound of Hayley's voice, folded in on itself. If she had no job, she'd have to go home with her mom.

"Try Kindle Trees, where Mike works. They're looking for shearers. Here's Mr. J." She heard Hayley tell him who she was.

"We're not busy enough yet, unless you do car repairs. You're next in line for working the counter," Jenkins said bluntly. "Check back at the end of the month."

"Okay," she said and hung up the wall phone in the kitchen. She looked up Kindle Tree Farms in the small directory.

The phone rang about seven times before a surly voice came on the line. "Kindle Trees. John speaking."

"I'm looking for summer work," she said in an unsure voice. She'd never sheared Christmas trees or done any other kind of manual labor outside of occasionally cutting the lawn. "I'm a friend of Mike Baxter."

"Name and age, please?" He sort of cackled. "It's hard work. We start at six, break for a half hour at eleven and quit at three. It don't matter who your friend is. What matters is if you can do the job."

She answered his questions.

"Be here on time tomorrow. Bring bug spray and wear a hat and gloves."

"Thanks," she said, but he had already hung up.

***

She was shoving her empty suitcase under the bed when she heard Hayley's voice. She nearly fell down the stairs getting to the kitchen, where her mom was asking Hayley about her year at Brown.

"Different. You know, everyone is so smart. I was the redneck from the backwoods." Hayley's gaze met Sarah's. "Hey, Sweeney. Bet it wasn't that way for you. Of course, you're not from the backwoods."

"Sounds sort of snobby," Sarah's mom said, reaching for a box of pasta on a high shelf.

Hayley got it for her. "Yeah, kind of, but cultured. These girls know opera and art and literature. I felt like a dope at first."

She and Sarah were grinning at one another. Can't-wait sort of grins, Sarah thought.

"I'll bet you showed them you were no dope."

"I spent a lot of time learning what they already knew."

Sarah's mom saw their smiles and looked sort of startled. "Why don't you two go for a swim? I'll be down soon."

Sarah jerked a thumb at the stairs. "Come on up. Got your suit?"

Hayley opened her shirt. Her bikini was no longer teeny tiny but somehow just as sexy. She filled it to the brim. They ran up the steps, shut Sarah's bedroom door quietly behind them and hugged.

"Can I stay over tonight and every night?" Hayley whispered.

Their foreheads touched, and Sarah breathed in Hayley's scent—suntan lotion and shampoo. "Mom is going home in two weeks. We'll be alone here until July."

Hayley's answer was a sly smile, and Sarah kissed it. "Can you wait?"

"No. I found a secluded spot. Come on, put your suit on. We'll sneak away."

CHAPTER SEVEN

2011

Sarah fell asleep over her book and awoke sluggishly when the phone rang. She answered without looking at the display.

"Hey, girlfriend. Thought this might be a good time to catch up with what's happening in Wisconsin. Actually, I thought it an excellent time for you to move to a state with two Democratic senators and a Democratic governor, all women."

"You caught me at a weak moment, Brook." Demonstrating in the cold was hard, especially at night. Hayley was far away.

"Why don't you come for a visit? I miss you."

She had hoped that Brook would move to Appleton after

graduation. Instead, she had taken a job in Washington State. "Sounds like a plan. If I lose my job, can you support me?" she asked teasingly.

"Free room and board as long as you want to stay."

"What happened to your live-in boyfriend?"

"He left me to be near Mount Hood."

"I'm so sorry." She should have kept closer contact with Brook. "My life revolves around protests in the cold. Next we'll be getting signatures for recall elections. We have to take back the senate to stop the governor's agenda. And then we'll be trying to recall him. And after that come the 2012 elections." There was no end to political demands on her time.

"You'll have a serious case of burnout. I've been watching Rachel Maddow. I know what's going on in Wisconsin. Aren't you tired? Don't you want more in your life?"

"Hayley turned up for a while. She's a reporter and a blogger."

Brook knew about Hayley. That first year at UW-Madison she had asked about the letters and whispered phone calls. Desperate to talk about Hayley, Sarah had broken the silence. She'd kept saying to herself "Shut up, shut up," even as she told Brook how she felt about Hayley. When she'd finally fallen silent, Brook had said, "I can't wait to meet her." Brook's understanding had cemented their friendship.

"You're shitting me. How was it?"

"A little like it used to be, but now she's back in New York."

"And you miss her," Brook said.

"I should never have let myself be taken in again."

"Yes, you should. You're not over her. Is she coming back?"

"I suppose she'll visit. Her family lives here. Tell me about Rex."

"Oh, it wasn't working out anyway. All he wanted to do was ski. I love to ski too, but it's a hobby, not a vocation. I miss him, though. It is nice to have someone to go places with, even though the only places he wanted to go were ski slopes."

They talked for another hour. That's how it was with Brook. They always had so much to say to each other. She vowed to do this more often.

***

Hayley and Sarah were standing on the sidewalk on Capitol Square, listening to the Democratic 14, as the senators had been dubbed. They had returned to the state a little over three weeks after they'd left—not because their paychecks had been withheld or their aides harassed—but because the union-stripping part of the Budget Repair Bill had been pulled for a vote. While the police tried to keep protesters out of the Capitol—they had been climbing in the windows—the bill had been passed Wednesday, March 9, without any Democratic amendments.

One of the Democratic senators said, "In the past few weeks, we awakened a sleeping giant," and the estimated crowd of a hundred thousand cheered. The senator was talking about the unions and the Democratic base.

She and Hayley had twice listened to Michael Moore and Jesse Jackson, who had visited Madison Saturday, March 12, along with Susan Sarandon. They had missed Sarandon's talk and gone looking for her but had never found her. They learned later she had spent most of her time talking to students.

"One of my all-time favorite stars," Hayley had moaned, "and I miss seeing her."

"Mom will be devastated. She loves Susan Sarandon."

The senators talked about their reasons for leaving the state and staying away—to force review and debate on the Budget Repair Bill, which was being rammed through the senate. Their attempts at compromise had failed. Now it was time to turn the massive protests into recalls.

The implications of the change in tactics ate away at Sarah. Would Hayley come back to report on recalls? Hayley was here for the huge protests. Going door-to-door collecting signatures was not exactly big news.

When the rally ended, they returned to the hotel. This time neither talked about taking the chill off with a cup of coffee or going out to eat. They went straight to bed, where they warmed each other. It was as if the weather that had conspired against the demonstrators brought them together.

"Hey, you're shaking." Hayley pulled her closer.

"When will I see you again?" Sarah asked. She'd told herself she wasn't going to talk about this. She was going to enjoy Hayley in the present and worry about the future later.

"You'll be so busy you won't miss me."

She pulled back to look into Hayley's eyes. "Are you kidding? You know how much non-fun it is to go door-to-door, asking for signatures? You could come and help. It would give you something to put on your blog."

"Maybe I will." Hayley kissed her with cool lips. She ran a chilly hand over Sarah's breasts and belly to the joining of her legs. Her cold fingers moved slowly, teasingly, until they became warm and slick.

Sarah lost her train of thought.

***

The governor's Biennial Budget Proposal was delayed till the Democratic 14 returned. The budget reduced school aid by $834 million. Property taxes were frozen, so if the savings on employee benefits and insurance failed to fill the hole in revenue jobs would have to be eliminated. It also reduced state aid to the University of Wisconsin System and UW-Madison by $250 million. Technical colleges lost over $71.6 million.

According to the governor, Wisconsin was broke and draconian cuts were necessary. However, during his first week in office he had proposed tax cuts for businesses that would increase the deficit by $80 million a year without any assurance that these cuts would add jobs. He had already turned down $800 million in federal stimulus funds for high-speed rail, sending those jobs out of state. He agreed to more stringent regulations for wind farms, causing a wind farm company to threaten to leave the state. Despite the governor's new slogan—"Wisconsin is Open for Business"—the governor was being picky about green jobs. So far there were no new jobs.

Sarah went with Jane and Margaret to collect recall signatures in Kaukauna on Saturday. She couldn't vote in the district they were targeting, but she could work for the recall of any senator. The library, where they picked up the petition papers and supposedly a list of friendly addresses, was crowded with volunteers.

They fanned out and covered both sides of the street. Margaret drove the car, while Jane and Sarah took opposite sides of the street. When Sarah came to a fenced-in yard with an unlocked gate, she didn't hesitate to walk up to the porch. After all, the address was on her sheet.

As she put her foot on the first step, a huge, hairy dog careened around the corner of the house. She froze, a scream stuck in her throat. The dog grabbed one leg of her jeans in its teeth and shook it, growling deep in its throat. The scream climbed out of her mouth.

"Thor, drop it!" a deep voice said sternly.

The dog stood back, tail wagging, tongue hanging out. Saliva dripped from its toothy smile.

"Good dog," the voice said, and Thor dropped to his haunches.

She looked up into the concerned face of a bearded man.

"That's how he plays," the man said. "Sorry if he scared you." He gestured toward the papers in her hands. "You got something for me to sign?"

"Recall papers for your senator," she squeaked, then cleared her throat and said it again.

"Good. Come on up. I'll sign them." When she glanced with trepidation at the dog, he said, "He's just a big puppy. He won't hurt you."

Later when she told Jane and Margaret, they laughed and laughed until she finally laughed with them. "I wet my pants," she admitted, and they all howled as if it was the funniest thing they ever heard.

***

This was not how she thought she'd be spending her weekends last fall before all this started. The upside to it, though, was having Hayley back in her life. At the apartment, she listened to her messages. Hayley's voice made the room seem emptier.

"Why don't you turn on your cell? I'm coming next weekend.

I'll go door to door with you. Meet me at the Outagamie Airport at seven twenty on Friday."

She spent the week trying hard to be patient with her students when all she wanted to do was speed up time. Tuesday and Wednesday nights she made phone calls. The people she called were supposedly part of the base and friendly to the cause, but Sarah talked to one man who told her he was never going to vote again. He trapped her on the phone as he went on and on about the broken system and how everyone was looking out for him or herself. She was feeling as if her life had been kidnapped when she got out of her car in front of her apartment that night, too tired to park in the garage.

Her heart nearly stopped when a tall man leaped out of a BMW convertible and caught up with her as she fumbled to unlock the outer door. She was wondering if she should run or scream or do both, but then he said, "Hey, have I changed that much?"

She looked at him. "Eddie?"

"I was in the area."

"But how did you...?" She opened the door and he followed her into the building.

"Easy. I called your mom. She said to say hi." In the dim hallway his teeth glistened. "I thought maybe we could get together."

"Well, sure," she said, although she longed to go to bed and read. She was in the middle of *The Help* and could hardly put it down. She had grabbed a peanut butter sandwich before leaving for the phone bank and was also hungry.

Although Eddie's pants still hung from his hips, his shoulders had broadened and his legs lengthened. He flipped his wavy, blondish hair out of his eyes and smiled at her. "You turned out pretty."

"Can I get you anything?" She eyed him suspiciously, remembering how he used to grab at her and Hayley and Beth. She could be cornered in here.

"Got any beer? I have a little weed." He fished a small plastic bag out of his pocket and waved it at her.

"Not tonight, Eddie. I have to work tomorrow."

"Do you mind if I smoke?"

She did mind and hesitated long enough for him to catch on. "Okay, okay. One beer and I'll go."

He sat down on her Danish modern couch, a relic dredged from the basement of her parents' old house. "So, how's it going? What are you doing with yourself?"

"Teaching. At least, that's what I'm doing now." Who knew what would happen? "How about you?"

"I work for a law firm in Milwaukee. Would you believe it?" He spread his arms. "I'm an attorney. I'll give you a break if you need my services."

She took two Leinenkugel Reds out of the fridge. "Want a peanut butter sandwich?"

"No thanks, and don't dirty a glass for me."

She handed him the bottle, made half a sandwich and sat down in the matching Danish chair.

"So, how are Beth and Hayley and Mike and Jeff?"

"Beth's a mama. She's also an attorney." Beth had always been the achiever in the family. She worked in their dad's firm, because that was the only place she could work a forty-hour week. "Hayley lives in New York. She's a journalist and a blogger. She came back to cover the protests." She took a bite of the sandwich. Peanut butter stuck to the roof of her mouth and she washed it down with beer. "Mike is an engineer and works for the DOT, and Jeff runs a fishing charter business in Florida."

He took a swig out of the bottle and sighed. "Ah, the protests. You must be involved in those, being a teacher."

She nodded, suddenly defensive. "Very."

"Hey, whatever works. Right?"

She relaxed a little. She was too tired to argue. The beer sliding down her throat soothed her.

Eddie glanced around the small apartment. "You must live alone, huh?"

"Yep."

He loosened his tie and grinned. "Would you like a little company tonight? I could sleep on the couch."

"Nope."

"I understand. Look, I'm going to be around tomorrow. I'll take you out to dinner. There are good restaurants downtown."

He chugged the rest of the beer, stood up and set the bottle on the short counter that separated the living room from the kitchenette.

"Yes, there are." She couldn't afford to go to them.

"I'll pick you up around six. What do you say?" He was standing near the door now, smiling at her. "For old time's sake."

"Sure. It'll be fun." Already she was wondering what in her limited wardrobe she would wear. She stood up but kept her distance from Eddie, half expecting him to try to draw her into an embrace.

When he closed the door behind him and she slid the dead bolt in place, she felt a rush of relief. Tomorrow she'd have more energy in case she had to fight him off, but she was surprised at how pleased she had been to see him. He brought back good memories from summers at the lake.

She fingered the phone, wanting to call Hayley and tell her Eddie had walked back into her life, but New York was an hour ahead of Wisconsin. She knew Hayley stayed up late, but Sarah was intimidated by Kristina, whom she'd never seen and probably never would. How stupid was that? Still, she went to bed without calling. Hayley would be here Friday. She'd have more news about Eddie to share then.

***

The next night she frowned at Eddie across the white tablecloth at the Wine Bar, unpleasantly surprised. "You're doing what?"

"Our firm is working on redistricting."

"Gerrymandering, you mean," she shot back.

"It's a job. Redistricting always follows the census and the party in power gets to do it. Besides, I'm pretty low on the totem pole."

She knew this about the census and redistricting, of course. Did he think she was an idiot? "You're going to change the districts so that the Democrats lose the next ten elections."

"I'd quit my job, but I have to pay for that BMW out there." He smiled and gestured toward the door.

"Eddie, there are more important things in life besides money."

"Tell me one. The bottom line is always about money. Every

war has been about money or oil or land. Every election is won by money."

She stared at him, knowing he was right, longing to go back to those summer days around the fire when everything had seemed so much simpler. She thought of how little control she'd had over her life then, but what kind of control did she have now?

"Let's not talk about it. I hate arguing with a pretty woman."

"That's sexist, Eddie," she said with disgust, and he threw his hands in the air as if pleasing her were impossible.

"Hey, I'm not a serious guy," he protested. "I'm not even a political guy."

That was the problem, of course. "Okay. Sorry. It's just that I am political."

Their plates were empty. She drank the rest of her wine and the waitress asked if they'd like dessert.

Eddie raised his brows and tilted his head at Sarah, and she had to laugh. He was incorrigible. "I'm stuffed. You have some."

He did and then paid the bill, giving the waitress a sizeable tip before they went out into the cool night. He opened the door for her, and she slid onto the low-slung leather seat.

"Nice place, Appleton, but not enough excitement for me," he commented as he got behind the wheel. "Would you like to see my room? It's right down the street at the Radisson. All the perks you could ask for."

She laughed. "You haven't changed, Eddie."

"At least let me light one up for you."

She probably would have said no to that too, but she didn't want to nix his every suggestion. They shared a smoke on the way back to the apartment, burning the shredded marijuana down to their fingertips in the parking lot. As always, it made her dizzy.

"Can I come in?" he asked with a smile and not much hope in his voice.

"No, but thanks for the night out. I can't afford to eat at the Wine Bar, so it was a real treat."

He galloped around the car, opened her door before she could and walked her to the outer door, waiting for her to unlock it before giving her a peck on the cheek.

Touched, she said, "Call me when you're in town again."

"You bet."

After she closed and locked her apartment door, she listened to her voice mail. "Hey, where are you tonight? You're always gone, and you never have your cell on."

She fingered her phone, but it was after ten in New York. If Hayley was home, Kristina might be too.

***

When Hayley strode through the gate at Outagamie Airport, Sarah was leaning against the wall across the wide aisle. Hayley veered toward her.

"Remember this isn't Madison," Sarah said.

Hayley gave her a big kiss on the mouth anyway. "We have to change the way people think."

She blushed.

"You know, that's what gives you away? If I were your sister, you wouldn't turn red." She winked at Sarah. "Why are you never home? Why do you not turn your cell on when you aren't?"

"Because it's rude to be talking on the phone when you're out with someone. Guess who took me to dinner last night? No, don't guess. Wait till we're in the car."

"Who? Susan Sarandon? Lena Taylor? Rachel Maddow?"

"Twelve questions." It was a game they had sometimes played when they were younger, usually about movie stars or characters in books or singers.

"Female?" Hayley headed for the door. "All I brought is in my backpack and computer case. I figured I could use your stuff if I forgot something—like my toothbrush." She laughed.

"Nope. Not female." It was cool and clear out, the sky loaded with stars. Sarah unlocked her car doors with her remote.

Hayley threw her backpack in the rear seat, and they climbed into the still-warm vehicle. She looked stumped. "Like Michael Moore or Ed Schultz?"

"Are you nuts? Why would any of those people want to have dinner with me?"

"Why would you want to have dinner with them? Am I having you for supper tonight?"

Sarah laughed. "No."

"I'm dying for a Wisconsin Friday night fish fry," Hayley said before guessing again, "Peter Barca or Jon Erpenbach?"

Sarah had hoped they could pick up a pizza and take it to the apartment and spend the night alone. "You've used up eight questions and you're not even close."

"My brother, Mike? Your dad? My dad? Your old flame? What was his name? Tim?"

"That's twelve." She was amazed that Hayley even remembered Tim.

Hayley was silent a moment, staring at her. "Fast Eddie?"

"Yeah. You got it."

"What's he doing? What does he look like? Does he still have a stash with him all the time?"

After listening to Sarah's answers, Hayley said, "Some people don't change."

"Oh, he's changed. I didn't know he was so cynical."

"More cynical than you and me?" Hayley asked with a crooked grin.

"He thinks everything comes down to the bottom line."

"Doesn't it?"

"We better eat before we go home. We may not get served after eight."

***

When they finally went to bed, the lump of deep fried food in Sarah's stomach was on the move. She lay quietly for a few moments. "Can we wait till morning?"

Hayley was up on one elbow, looking down at her. Disappointment flitted across her face. "What?"

"You fell asleep the first night we were together."

"Is this payback?"

"This is about being too full."

Hayley fell back and whooped with laughter. "This is about gas," she finally managed to say. "Let's talk. Do you think these recalls have a chance of succeeding?"

"Sure. Think of all the demonstrators. People are furious."

"How many signatures do you have to get?"

"Twenty-five percent of the votes cast for the governor in the last election."

"In that district?"

"Think so. Oh, and that senator has to be in office for at least a year."

Hayley's voice was already thickening. Her body jerked in reflex. She threw an arm around Sarah. "I missed you, babe," she said just before her breathing evened out into a low snore.

"That was a short conversation."

"Long day," Hayley muttered.

***

In confusion Sarah searched for the ringing phone. It lay among the sheets. Outside the window, the waning moon cast its light across the carpet. She glanced at the clock—3:05 a.m. Who could be calling? Her mom? Her dad?

Hayley dragged her head off the pillow as Sarah said, "'Lo."

"Who is this?" a woman asked.

"Who *is* this?" Sarah said indignantly, her voice slurred by sleep.

"Kristina Berken. Why are you answering Hayley's phone?"

"Because it's ringing?" she said with asperity. "Why are you calling at three in the morning?"

"None of your business. Put Hayley on."

Sarah handed Hayley the cell and fell back on the pillow. Why hadn't she noticed the different ring? Why was the phone on in the first place? Her heart was pounding. She was wide-awake and angry.

"Yeah. Sarah is a childhood friend. You know that. Of course, I'm staying with her. You scared us. Why are you calling at this time of the night?"

There was a long pause, while Hayley fell back on the pillow and listened. Her tone was different when she talked to Kristina, sort of conciliatory. "Okay. I'll find another place. No problem. You and Rob need your privacy."

She turned off the phone and threw it down. "Damn. She does this at least once a month."

Sarah said, "I'm sorry. I just grabbed it without thinking."

"I forgot to turn it off, but now that we're awake, how about a little fun?"

"You could move back here and live with me. Of course, I might not have a job." She didn't really believe that, though.

Hayley covered her, holding her down. When Sarah offered no resistance, she buried her face in Sarah's neck and made a rude noise, then said, "How about a little struggle?"

Sarah tried halfheartedly to free herself and gave up, laughing. "Okay. Have your way with me."

"I will." As soon as she let go of Sarah's hands, though, Sarah flipped her and they ended up in a heap on the floor.

That was when they heard the knocking on the door. They jumped to their feet. "Who's there?" Sarah called in a wobbly voice.

"Me. Eddie. I need a place to lay my head."

Sarah exchanged a surprised glance with Hayley before they grabbed their clothes and pulled them on. She was about to open the door when she thought to ask Eddie why he wasn't at the Radisson.

"It's a long story and it's cold out in the car."

She unlocked the door and peered through the opening. It was Eddie all right. His tie was askew and his shirt unbuttoned partway down his chest. She opened up enough for him to stagger inside. He smelled strongly of marijuana.

"Hey, look who's here," he said, eyeing Hayley.

Sarah said with alarm, "You stink, Eddie. Are the cops on your tail?"

"Nope. I gave them the slip."

"Go get your suitcase, Eddie. You're going to have to put your clothes in the car," Hayley said. "Just in case."

He reeled out the door. A few moments later, they heard him banging down the hall with his suitcase. Hayley went out to take it from him.

"We ought to send him away, you know," Sarah said. "I'll lose my job if he gets caught here. Hell, we may end up in jail with him."

"Say the word and I'll make him go."

She hesitated and he slipped into the apartment. While he showered, Hayley took the smelly suit out to the car, holding it at arm's length.

They were sitting side by side on the couch when Eddie came out of the bathroom. His wet hair curled around his rather large ears.

"God, my mama used to wait up for me like this," he said, dropping into the chair. "Can't we just go to bed?"

"Sure," Hayley said. "If you get Sarah into trouble, I'll haunt you, though."

"I was in someone else's room. I just decided it was better not to go back to my own."

Sarah tossed her only spare blanket on the couch. He would have to use the throw pillows. In bed again, she and Hayley whispered in the silvery moonlight. They had silent sex, all the more exciting because Eddie was in the other room.

"Like hiding in the sand among the pines," Hayley said afterward.

Eddie drank three cups of coffee in the morning, ate three eggs and two pieces of toast. He had work to do, he said. "Sorry about last night, but thanks for letting me crash." He studied the two of them across the small dining table. "You two are still the best of friends, huh?"

"Yes, Eddie, we are," Hayley said.

"My grandpa died and my dad sold the cabin," he told them.

"I knew it was sold," Sarah said. "Sorry about your grandpa."

"Those summers were some of the best times of my life."

Sarah wondered how she'd feel if the summer home of her childhood was sold. Her mother would have to die first, and that was not something she could think about. "I'm sorry. I can't imagine not having a place on the lake."

His pale eyes looked smeary in the sunshine pouring through the window. He ran a hand over them as if to clear his vision.

"You ought to stop using," Sarah said.

"Don't tell me you never smoke the stuff." He looked at Hayley.

"I do a lot of blogging at night. I have to be able to think." She tapped her temple.

He slapped the table. "Gotta go."

"Checking out the new redistricting lines?"

"Something like that. Have to meet with a few people."

"Don't screw it up too much," Sarah said.

"We don't want it to end up in the courts." He winked at her. "Can't you two spare a hug for an old friend?"

They hugged him at the door. "I'll call when I'm back," were his last words.

"Do we have to hit the pavement now?" Hayley said. It was after nine. Outside clouds scudded across the blue sky.

"Not till after we shower."

"Let's get down and dirty first," Hayley said with a grin. She didn't seem worried about Kristina's phone call.

Sarah asked if she was really going to have to look for a new place to live as they drove to pick up the petition papers from the back room of a bar in Kaukauna.

"She usually backs off."

Sarah asked, "Why would she throw you out for staying with a childhood friend?"

"She knows you're more than that, but I can't afford to fly back and forth like I've been doing, Sarah. The newspaper pays me a pittance. The advertising for the blog has fallen off."

Sarah actually felt nauseated, even though this was not unexpected news. "Don't you miss the lake? Don't you ever want to come home?"

"I miss you."

"I don't think I could stand it if we no longer had our place on the lake. It's my retreat from reality."

"You didn't grow up in the boonies with gun-crazed boys. Besides, our place is on the back road."

"You have lake access." She parked outside the bar, not ready to end this conversation although she knew it was a hopeless one.

Hayley met her puzzled gaze. "Look. From the time I started junior high I wanted to get out of there. You were my saving grace. Knowing you were coming back in the summer kept me from going completely crazy."

That Hayley wanted to run from the one place Sarah loved most was just not something she could accept without an argument. The pain in her chest was affecting her breathing. "So you wouldn't care if your parents sold their home and moved to Florida?"

"Only if it meant I'd never see you again," Hayley said with a sad smile.

"I want to live there some day."

Hayley covered Sarah's hand with her own. "Come on, let's go collect signatures."

The lone woman in the empty back room, the one dispensing the petitions and names and addresses, had no maps of the area. "Go out the back door here and you'll be on Second Street. When you finish with those addresses, there is an apartment complex across the bridge."

"Okay," Sarah said, thinking next time she'd bring the phone book with its maps.

They started off. The houses were modest, set on a ridge close to the sidewalk, often with broken cement steps leading up to rickety porches. Even the sidewalk was broken. They avoided the yards with fences. They rang a few doorbells and pounded on those without. In every case, someone came to the door and told them they'd already signed.

"Somebody has already done this street," Sarah said the obvious. "Maybe we should go over to the apartments."

After knocking on apartment doors for forty-five minutes, they returned to the bar. "We got two signatures. Most people have already signed."

"Probably ones missed the first time around," the woman said. "Do you want to go out to one of the subdivisions? You might get more signatures there." She was flipping through the addresses. "How about this one? I know how to get there."

They parked at the end of a block and walked from door to door as Sarah had done with Jane and Margaret. The sun shone through a veil of thin clouds, but few people were outside. They did not stop at the addresses that were not on the list. One house was set far back from the sidewalk, looking deserted and unkempt, with a dog roaming the front yard.

"We're not going to that door," Sarah said firmly, when Hayley hesitantly put a foot in the driveway. "Come on, let's walk to the end of the street and turn back." They had covered most of the territory, which had long stretches between houses.

On their way back to the bar they passed a house that had been trashed by the tornado that had hit earlier in the week. A woman was sifting through the wreckage. A man carrying a clipboard and dressed in a suit stood on the grass nearby.

"Stop," Hayley said urgently, and Sarah screeched to a halt. "What the hell happened here?"

"Tornado. Didn't I tell you about it?" Had she?

Hayley got out of the car and picked her way through the debris toward the woman. "Can I help?" she asked as Sarah trailed behind her.

The woman's hair was tangled, and she was dressed in torn jeans and a ragged sweatshirt. She gave the appearance of someone who has nothing when she turned a twisted smile on Hayley and said, "How can you help? I lost everything." She pointed at a house across the street. "They weren't touched. What did I do?"

"Tell me what you're looking for and my friend and I will search too."

"Who the hell are you anyway? Do you live around here?"

Hayley glanced at Sarah, who was eyeing the next-door neighbor's house where the corner of the garage had collapsed. "My friend does."

"We've already gone through this stuff two, three times. There are nails everywhere. I don't want to get sued on top of everything. I'm looking for anything we missed, anything salvageable." She turned to the man with the clipboard. "You got everything you need?"

"Yes. We'll send you a check."

The woman, who might have been anywhere between thirty- and forty-something, bent to her task. After assuring her they would never sue, Hayley carefully moved shreds of boards and drywall. Sarah found herself drawn into what seemed a futile act. However, when she uncovered an intact teapot, she excitedly held it aloft. "Want this?"

The woman's head snapped up. "Put it over there." She pointed at a small pile of items piled on the grass.

Enthused by the find, Sarah moved among the wreckage,

using both hands to sift through the clutter. She found a bedraggled photograph book and glanced through it. The photos were water-spotted, the pages damp and curling. She showed the album to the woman, who came hopping through the trash to her side. Blood was running down one of her ankles.

She took the album from Sarah and looked through it, wiping her eyes and nose with the sleeve of the sweatshirt. "Where did you find this?" she demanded, and when Sarah showed her, she began digging in the area. None of them wore gloves.

Sarah grabbed the moment to throw Hayley a meaningful look and point to her watch. It was nearly five.

Hayley, though, apparently wanted to keep on with this quest. She eventually came up with a jewelry box that looked like it had been on the *Edmund Fitzgerald*. "Look at this," she yelled excitedly.

"Hey, my childhood treasure chest," the woman again slogged through the dangerous rubble to examine Hayley's find.

Sarah took this opportunity to carefully make her way to Hayley's side and whisper, "We should go turn in these papers."

"What papers?" the woman asked. "You been spying on me?"

"Recall petitions."

"That's why you're here. I knew there was a reason. Well, you can just go now. I have relatives coming over tomorrow to help."

Hayley said, "Hey, that's all we wanted to do. We're sorry about your house."

"Everybody's got an agenda." The woman's fists rested on her hips. "I don't have time for politics right now."

"It wasn't an agenda," Hayley protested.

"Go see the guy across the street. He'll sign. I'm okay with either one. I just want my house back, and they aren't going to give me that."

Sarah and Hayley picked their way out of the rubble and walked through the longish grass and across the street, where they rang and knocked to no avail. Before they drove away, Hayley called and waved to the woman, who without looking urged them on their way with a backhanded gesture.

"One good reason never to buy a house," Hayley said as Sarah turned the corner.

"She wasn't the friendliest person. I mean, there we were getting all torn up looking for her stuff."

"Do you blame her? I don't think she was angry with us. You had a tornado come through this week and never said anything about it?"

She remembered the walls of driving rain. "The tornado didn't hit us, but I couldn't see through the rain, it was so dense."

"I think she was mad because it was her house that was trashed and not the ones around it."

"That's a tornado for you. Picky."

"Let's go to your apartment and spend the rest of our time together."

Sarah grinned. "My thoughts exactly. Why did you want to stop in the first place? We weren't supposed to bother the people who were hit by the storm."

"I had the sudden urge to do something nice. It doesn't happen very often. I'll do something nice to you."

Sarah laughed. "I promise to be more appreciative."

"What comes after this?" Hayley asked when they dropped the petitions off at the bar.

"Getting out the vote. Phone calls, canvassing. We've got candidates."

At the apartment they showered together, washing off the bloody dirt left by nail scrapes and sharp-edged boards. As the water cascaded down on them, Hayley pushed Sarah up against the far wall where they slid slowly down to the porcelain floor of the tub.

That night Hayley sat at Sarah's little table and wrote about getting recall signatures. Sarah massaged her shoulders and read over her shoulder.

These were dedicated volunteers, Hayley wrote, *the same people who had protested in the cold and snow in Madison during February and March.* She went on to tell how volunteers had presented petition papers at one recall senator's door, only to be told by his wife that he now lived with his young mistress in Madison. His wife had signed. Hayley retold the story about Sarah and the dog that attached itself to her jeans. And, of course, she embellished their search that afternoon for memorabilia at the house that had been trashed by the tornado.

"You've got to keep it interesting. Otherwise, you're not going to get any readers." Hayley looked up at her with a smile that filled her with longing. Tomorrow she would fly back to New York, and who knew when she'd see her again.

After devouring a salad and pizza, they sat on the couch and ate chunky chocolate ice cream. When Hayley's phone rang, she glanced at the display and turned it off.

"I can come maybe once a month," she said, her pupils huge in her pale green eyes.

"Why can't I come to you once a month too?" Sarah asked.

"Where would we stay? Can you afford a hotel room in New York?"

"Don't you have other friends?"

"Yeah, but it's hard to keep a secret."

"You said I wasn't a secret."

"You're the best secret in the world." Hayley leaned forward to plant an ice cream kiss on Sarah's lips, but Sarah turned her head and it landed on her cheek, a sticky memento of where she stood in Hayley's life.

No fights, she told herself. She knew she wasn't a secret, that what they did together was supposedly the secret. She told herself to let it go. Arguing just left her feeling estranged and lonely with no way to make up after Hayley left. She wiped the ice cream off with the back of her hand and licked it before returning the kiss.

***

At the airport the next day as she watched the jet taxi down the runway, she was glad she'd held her tongue. Despite the lack of control she had over this most important part of her life, she swallowed the bitterness. She had a choice. She could send Hayley out of her life or cherish what little time she had with her, even if she only saw her once a month. No one else had come close to taking her place in the past eleven years.

CHAPTER EIGHT

Summer and Autumn 1998

"I'll be down in a few minutes," Sarah's mom said as the two girls slipped out the side door carrying beach towels and bags with books and suntan lotion.

"So much for the secluded spot," Sarah said as they hurried down the path toward the lake. "We can't slip away now."

"Eddie will probably find us and then we won't get away till tonight."

Summer and Eddie were becoming synonymous. "Can Mike pick me up tomorrow? I'm going to shear trees."

Hayley stopped her headlong rush to the water, and Sarah ran into her. "The first week nearly kills Mike. He always threatens to quit and falls in bed right after supper."

"Well, you and I can fall in bed together, since it's the only job I could find. I'll have to go back home with Mom if I don't have a job." She worried, though, about whether she could swing a machete all day long with the sun beating down while fighting off mosquitoes and biting flies. She'd heard Mike talk about what it was like to shear trees.

She dragged her toes in the sand, relishing its warmth. On Memorial Day weekend, her family had come up and put in the pier and now she and Hayley ran to its end and dove in the water. Sarah swam to the surface and let out a whoop. The warm day made the water feel cool.

Sarah's mom waded in, pausing every foot or so to accustom herself to the temperature. Sarah remembered her diving off the pier not so many years ago. Finally, she thrust forward in a breaststroke accompanied by a gasp.

When they emerged from the water, Sarah's mother wrapped up in a beach towel and sat in one of the three chairs Sarah and Hayley had gotten out of the boathouse. She opened her book.

The girls glanced at each other. "We're going for a walk, Mom," Sarah said.

Her mother waved them off, and they ran down the beach, towels waving behind them, and disappeared into a grove of trees. Sarah heard her heart pounding in her ears, felt it pumping in her throat. Alive with anticipation, her skin tingled with the warmth of sun, the heat of the sand, the soft breeze.

Ahead of her, Hayley dropped her towel and fell in a laughing heap on top of it. Sarah spread her own and dropped to her knees. "What a great find," she said, looking around. The hiding place was a small patch of sand, only big enough for the two of them. It was surrounded by white pines. The lake could be heard but not seen.

They succumbed to impatient desire. There was little nuance in their lovemaking. Their kisses were bruising, their fingers quickly thrust into bikini bottoms. Sarah's climax was a startling release, and she would have cried out had Hayley not put her hand over her mouth.

"I know it's hard, but you have to be quiet."

They clung to each other, but as the sun penetrated the pines, they grew hot and fell apart. When their breathing slowed, Hayley rose on an elbow and tugged at Sarah's swimsuit. "Take it off." She began removing her own, her uncovered skin a shocking contrast against her tan.

"What if someone finds us?" Sarah said, holding back.

"No one's going to find us."

"Eddie might come looking."

"Eddie doesn't get out of his boat during the day except to ski." Already nude, Hayley helped Sarah wriggle out of her suit and pulled her close. "There, that's better. Relax."

It was only when they started again, more slowly this time, that Sarah forgot the unthinkable consequences that awaited them if they were caught.

***

Mike picked Sarah up at five forty the next morning. She'd been waiting for ten minutes, standing bleary-eyed on the front porch dressed in shorts and an old T-shirt—hat and gloves in hand. She carried a backpack with suntan lotion and fly and mosquito spray and a bagged lunch. Afraid they'd be late and she'd be out of a job, she jumped in the vehicle and slammed the door.

Mike's old truck peeled out of the two-rut driveway, spraying sand in its wake. "I fell back asleep. Sorry."

"Hey, thanks for not forgetting me."

He shot a glance at her as he stepped on the gas again when they hit the county road. "If you can get through the first few days, you'll be okay. Spray good." Mike looked like Hayley. The same light green eyes and coppery hair. He was the color of mahogany from his many hours in the sun. Her skin was fair. Belatedly, she realized she should have worn a long-sleeved shirt.

At the tree farm, John asked one of the guys—all the workers were young—to demonstrate how to shear a pine and a spruce. The trees were supposed to be symmetrical, the base approximately two-thirds as wide as the height. She had no clue how she was going to judge that. After he passed out shearing knives to the crews, the shearers piled onto a flatbed truck. They were taken to one of several fields. Mike and Sarah were dropped off in an area planted with Douglas firs, which were all around six feet—a stretch for her.

Sarah hadn't thought much about how heavy the shearing knife would feel after swinging it for an hour, although it was probably lighter than a machete. She tried to economize her moves, like Mike did, but after that first hour, she began using both hands, shaping the tree carefully, falling further and further behind Mike until she could no longer see him. When she reached the end of the first row, she stopped to slather herself with another layer of sunblock and spray away the flies and mosquitoes that maddeningly circled and landed on her—their stings like tiny electric shocks.

Long before the break, she thought she would never get through the day. Her arms each weighed more than her body. Sweat rolled down her face into her eyes, but it was futile to wipe it away because it just came back. When she reached the road again, there was no sign of Mike. She took her break alone at eleven and never saw Mike until the truck picked them up at three. She heard the horn and ran, stumbling toward the sound with legs trembling and arms leaden with fatigue.

Mike reached out a hand and pulled her atop the flat bed. "You fucking did it."

She grinned, her face stiff with sunburn and dried sweat and said proudly, "I fucking did, didn't I?"

None of the new people were talking. They slumped forward as she did, zombie-like. Her joints felt impossibly stretched and her aching muscles cramped. She wasn't sure she could jump off the truck, but when they stopped at Kindle's building, Mike put out a hand for her. She steadied herself against him.

He grinned, looking dirty and beat. "Hey, you done good. Tomorrow is the toughest day."

She was too tired to respond with more than a weak smile. She hadn't thought beyond getting through this first day, hadn't considered the second one. When he dropped her off at the lake and she entered the kitchen, her mom gasped.

"Poor baby," she said, her fingers hovering but not quite touching Sarah's face and arms. "We need to get some aloe on you."

Her mom led her to the nearest bathroom and gently bathed her face and arms, which Sarah now saw were burned badly and covered with bites and black tree sap. "I should have worn a long sleeve shirt." She sat on the toilet lid and closed her eyes.

"You don't have to do this, you know," her mom said.

"Yeah, I do," she said, not sure why quitting wasn't an option. "I'm going to put my suit on." She thought the lake water would soothe her skin.

"I don't know if that's a good idea. You'll get more burned."

The water felt cold against the heat of her body, and she didn't stay in long. She went upstairs, where the shower shot painful pellets at her. When the soap felt like sandpaper, she finally realized how burned she was. She pulled an undershirt and shorts over her still wet skin.

Her mom was waiting outside the door and after Sarah lay down, she smeared more aloe on her burns. Sarah lay on her back with arms and legs spread and drifted in and out of sleep. When she heard Hayley's voice, she peered through slits.

The mattress shifted as Hayley sat on the edge.

"Don't touch me," she warned.

"Not even here?" Hayley slid a hand in her shorts.

"My mom might come back."

"I'll just lie down and you can tell me what it's like to shear trees."

"Your brother is Superman."

Hayley laughed softly. "He thinks he is, but he was a sissy in the beginning. He cried after his first day."

"Well, I could cry thinking about tomorrow."

When she woke up again, her mom was standing over her. "Dinner's ready, sweetie. You need to eat."

She sat up. "Where's Hayley?"

"She left. Said she'd meet you at the campfire."

She staggered downstairs and ate the chicken leg with mashed potatoes and fresh green beans her mom put in front of her, washing the food down with milk. No beer tonight, she thought.

"I wish you wouldn't go back," her mom said.

She grunted. "I just have to get through the next few days."
She wondered if that were possible.

Hayley showed up again after dark, her voice piercing a
painful dream. "Aren't you coming to the campfire?"

"Not tonight. Tell Mike I'll be waiting on the porch at five
thirty."

"He's already in bed. See you tomorrow afternoon."

Sarah opened her eyes. "You're not staying the night."

"Nope."

She didn't have the strength to ask her not to go.

"I'll drink a beer for you." And then she was gone.

***

The next morning Sarah wore an old long sleeve shirt over
her T-shirt and jeans. Her face was shiny with sunscreen. She
had darkened her swollen eyelids with makeup and hung her
sunglasses around her neck. This time she would tie her mother's
sun hat under her chin tightly and not let it dangle.

The truck dropped her off with Mike at a plantation of white
and Scotch pines. The day was warming up fast, and mosquitoes
and deer flies lit on her even as she sprayed her arms and legs. She
lifted the shearing knife on the first tree, and pain shot through
her biceps and shoulders. But she slashed carefully, shaping
the tree into a perfect inverted V on all sides. She noticed the
misshapen trunks that previous shearings had caused. She even
imagined the trees feeling pain, maybe because her own agony
was so great that sometimes tears ran down her cheeks. The salty
deposits attracted flies.

At eleven Mike was again long out of sight, and she lay down
on the bed of needles between the trees while she ate her sandwich.
She wakened with a start when she was bitten on the cheek by a
deerfly. Staggering to her feet, she continued down the row.

The rest of the week dragged on as if the days were eighteen
hours long, instead of nine. They spent a half hour getting to the
trees and back again and were off the half hour for lunch. Her
shoulder and elbow joints felt as if they might be permanently

damaged. Her arms and back ached. She'd protected herself from further sunburn, and although she never got used to the bugs circling her head, she sprayed enough sometimes to gag herself. She'd probably die of these overdoses someday, but right now she didn't care. She just wanted to kill the buggers. At home, she ate and fell in bed.

Friday Mike gave her a hand up to the flatbed. "You fucking made it through the week. I was betting on you and I won."

"Is there any money in this?"

"You bet." He handed her a ten. "You fucking deserve it."

He only used the f-word around the guys, she'd noticed. She tried to hand the money back, but he put up his hands until she said, "For gas." After all, he picked her up and took her home.

She swam that afternoon, feeling the healing heat of the sun on her sore shoulders. Hayley joined her, diving off the end of the pier and coming up under her, touching her body as she rose to the surface.

"You did it."

She felt inordinately proud and pulled Hayley under where she kissed her. When they later wandered over to the campfire, she drank a warm beer and conked out in the sand. Hayley had to guide her steps home, where she climbed into bed with a beery sigh and only woke up as she came to a climax under Hayley's touch. She saw it was morning—six o'clock.

"I'll be back." She peed and brushed her teeth before tiptoeing back to bed, where she returned Hayley's favor.

They slept till ten when Sarah's mother tapped on the door and said breakfast was waiting—a breakfast as big as Sarah's appetite, which had expanded through the week. Then they cleaned up after themselves and went down to the lake.

Eddie was waiting along with Mike. The towrope jerked painfully on Sarah's sore joints, but she skied anyway. Eddie tossed her a beer when she climbed back in the boat, but she threw it back with a shake of the head and dropped into one of the backseats to spot Mike. She saw herself as someone who could do anything—anything physical anyway.

***

When her second year at UW-Madison started, Sarah moved into an apartment with Brook. At first she wrote and called Hayley every day, but after she found a job entering data for the UW-Madison Engineering Department, there was less free time. Between work, classes and the shopping and cooking that she and Brook shared, she walked miles every week, and the homework quickly piled up. Hayley admitted to being snowed under too, and sometimes days passed without any communication between them.

One day she came home from work to the small, seedy apartment and found Brook studying with a friend. "Hey, it's my roomie, Sarah Sweeney. Sarah, this is Chandler Hastings."

Chandler wore her hair in a long braid down her back from which small wisps escaped. Her eyes were gray, her skin smooth and her lips full. She took Sarah in with a level look. "Brook says you're an English major. I almost chose that myself."

"Yeah?" Sarah said. "I picked up crabmeat rangoons and sushi. Anyone want to share?"

"Me," Brook said, raising a hand.

"I've got to go." Chandler unfolded long legs. "See you soon."

When she was gone, Brook said, "I wish I had those long legs." She dipped a rangoon in sweet and sour sauce and popped it into her mouth. "Yum. Thanks for getting these."

"It's so easy to make you happy."

"I know. Good food, good friends and good grades."

Sarah raised her brows. "And Ken." Brook's on and off again boyfriend. Curious, she asked about Chandler.

"She comes from a small farm in Iowa near Ames. She has an autistic brother. She sits next to me in two of my classes, and she fixed my bike tire. She even drives tractors."

"Interesting," Sarah said. Her dad had insisted his kids learn how to change a tire after a girl in Beth's class disappeared. He didn't want his girls kidnapped by someone who stopped to help. It turned out that the girl had run away with her boyfriend, though—not taken by some sexual predator.

Chandler was there again the next day when Sarah returned from work. She and Brook were eating popcorn and tossing questions back and forth. "Hey, there's more popcorn in the pan," Brook said.

She heard them laughing when she went into the kitchen. Brook's giggle was contagious, and Sarah joined them, throwing herself in the ancient easy chair from which puffs of dust arose. "Wish studying was that much fun."

"Chandler was telling me about this kid who tried to elbow her way out of class on her belly." Her laughter rippled like music.

"Did she get out the door without being stopped?" What kid would risk the ridicule of classmates?

"I don't know. It happened in my brother's class."

"A special class?" she asked and then worried that she shouldn't have said "special."

"Not really. They mainstream these kids. Sometimes classes are just too long to hold their attention."

Sarah went to her room to study, but she found herself trying to hear what Brook and Chandler were saying. She closed her door and tried to concentrate. She was studying the derivatives of words, a mind-numbing task. She wished she could escape it by crawling out of the room. When Brook tapped on the door and popped her head inside, she woke up feeling guilty.

"Aha! Caught you catnapping. Want to go party?"

It was all she needed to hear. She leaped out of bed, suddenly full of energy. "Where?" she thought to ask as the three of them went out the door.

"My neighborhood block party," Chandler said.

It was a Friday and the party was already raging. Students filled the sidewalks, drinking beer and eating junk food. A campus policeman strolled among them, checking IDs. Those who were underage stashed their drinks under bushes or handed them to older friends.

Brook hooked up with Ken, an amiable junior who was majoring in chemical engineering. Despite his dreamy, myopic eyes and perpetual slump, Sarah thought he was kind of cute in a nerdy way. He was certainly smart. Brook was less enthusiastic, confessing only that he was funny and reliable.

Chandler steered Sarah to two vacated chairs. Her roommates

came over and she introduced them. "Want to see our place?" she asked when they wandered off.

"Sure," she said, not wanting to be rude.

They clambered up the narrow stairs to the second floor. Two bikes stood in the landing. There was nothing special about the place, and Sarah was wondering why she had invited her here when Chandler asked if she wanted to watch a video with her Sunday night.

"Is Brook coming?" she asked.

"Well, no."

She was wondering how she would tell Brook when Chandler explained, "Brook knows I was going to ask you."

"Oh," was all she could think to say. "What's the movie?"

"What would you like to see?"

She almost told her about Hayley, but Chandler's worried gray eyes kept her mum. With a twinge of guilt, she said, "You pick. Sounds like fun."

That first date was shared with Chandler's roommates, who wandered in and out of the sitting room either singularly or with their dates. Kathy Wolcroft watched the entire movie with them—which was *Wait Until Dark*. Sarah was riveted to the small screen, experiencing angst even though she knew Audrey Hepburn was going to outwit the villain.

Before the movie, Chandler had made a big bowl of popcorn, out of which everyone who passed through scooped handfuls. Halfway through, she paused for intermission and made more. Together she and Sarah drank a six-pack of Leinie's Red.

Chandler insisted on walking her back to her apartment. They crunched through piles of dry leaves even as freshly falling ones drifted down. "Like the movie?"

"Pretty scary."

"Let's do this again. Okay?"

She hesitated, almost brought up Hayley's name and then decided not to. She still considered Hayley going to Brown as a betrayal. They could be watching videos together and sharing a bed. "Sure. Want to come to my place next Sunday?"

"That would be cool. Surprise me with the movie."

***

Sarah invited Hayley for homecoming weekend. She had tickets for the football game and afterward there would be partying in the streets, especially if the Badgers won. Hayley flew in Friday afternoon. Sarah borrowed Ken's car to pick her up—an old Camaro that made almost as much noise as a plane. When Hayley smiled at her, green eyes glowing and hair hanging in thick coppery waves around her shoulders, she felt such a surge of love that she forgot everything, including how she planned to explain Hayley to Chandler, who assumed Hayley was nothing more than a good friend.

She had solved an embarrassing situation by enlisting Brook and Ken and turning the threesome for the game into five, which multiplied into four more when two of Chandler's roommates and their boyfriends decided to join them. They went to games en-masse anyway. When Chandler wanted to come to the airport, she'd said a firm no.

In Ken's car they could say little over the roar of the engine. Sarah was feeling shy anyway and hated the distance she sensed between them, a space filled with unshared memories and experiences. "Thanks for coming," she finally said as she parked in the small lot behind Ken's apartment, a couple doors down the street from hers.

"What?" Hayley said loudly before the engine died. In the sudden quiet she gave Sarah a wicked grin. "How am I going to keep my hands off you, Sweeney?"

The tempo of Sarah's heart sped up. "And who said you had to?"

Brook and Chandler were waiting when they reached the apartment. Sarah introduced Chandler as a friend, which was true. The plan was to go out as soon as Ken and Kathy and her boyfriend showed up.

"Excuse us for a minute," Hayley said when Sarah showed her where to put her backpack. She dragged Sarah into her bedroom, shut the door behind them and leaned against it.

Sarah caught a glimpse of Chandler's surprised face before the door shut. She didn't want to hurt her. She knew she should have told her about Hayley. She was just a moral coward, but right now all she wanted was to be alone with Hayley.

"Why is that girl here? Do we have to hang around these people?" Hayley asked before kissing her soundly.

"You mean Chandler? She's a friend, and Brook, my roomie, is my best friend. She's the only one who knows about us."

"I thought I was your best friend," Hayley said, looking very serious before kissing Sarah's nose and ears.

"You are, but you're not around. Besides, don't you want to see Madison? It's an exciting place."

"Not if it interferes with our time together."

She and Hayley got smashed that night. Sarah hardly remembered falling into bed. When she awoke in the night, Hayley was lying flat on her back, snoring. Sarah started a caress but lacked the energy to continue and fell asleep instead. She awoke to daylight and voices outside the bedroom.

One look at her watch induced a moan. A headache was crowding her skull. It was close to ten. No time for even a quickie. Someone was knocking on the door. "We just woke up. We'll be out in a minute."

"Hey, we'll meet you at Chandler's in an hour," Brook said.

Sarah held her breath till the front door closed and footsteps receded on the stairs. She hopped out of bed, peered cautiously out the door and motioned for Hayley to follow. They showered together, made quick love and arrived at Chandler's apartment within a few minutes of the hour.

Chandler moped through the football game, which the Badgers won, and through the rest of the evening as they partied. They ended up on the pier that jutted out into Lake Mendota at the Union, lying on their backs, looking at the crystal clear sky with its zillions of stars.

"Reminds me of summer nights at the lake," Sarah said nostalgically, thinking that she and Hayley could be doing this every weekend if Hayley hadn't gone to Brown.

"Except it's colder." They were snuggled together next to Ken and Brook, all of them keeping each other warm. Chandler had disappeared a while ago, as had Kathy and her boyfriend. The partying in the streets could still be heard.

The next day she drove Hayley around campus in Ken's car. "What's going on with you and Chandler?" Hayley asked as her fingers wormed their way into Sarah's crotch, causing her to go through a red light. Horns blared.

"I can't drive and deal with lust at the same time," Sarah said, "and I can't afford a ticket."

"You're avoiding the question."

"Nothing is going on, Hayley. I just need to see you once in a while to reinforce us."

"I've been thinking that maybe we should give each other a little free rein when we're not together."

"What does that mean?" Sarah asked, knowing well what it meant. Hayley wanted to get it on with others. It hurt to breathe.

"I'll always love you best," Hayley said with complete seriousness.

Her eyes filled with tears, and she would have rear-ended someone had Hayley not called out with alarm, "Hey, sweetie, watch where you're going!" She added, "We better not talk about this. Okay?"

"No. I want to know what you mean."

"Just that it's okay if we date other people." Hayley shrugged a shoulder. "Isn't that what everybody advises? Experiment a little. We'll come back to each other."

"And what if we don't?" She nearly sideswiped parked vehicles because she kept glancing at Hayley. The word "experiment" could only mean one thing—sex.

"You have to believe we will."

"Is there an us?" She was crying now, knowing what a mistake that was. She didn't want Hayley's pity.

Hayley wiped the tears away with a wadded tissue. "Don't, Sarah. We had such a good time."

She sniffed them back and pushed Hayley's hand away. "I'm okay. I suppose you're sleeping with someone." She wondered if it was a boy or girl.

They made up before Hayley boarded the plane, locked in a bathroom stall, kissing and whispering endearments.

It was a warning Sarah chose to ignore.

CHAPTER NINE

Summer 2011

That homecoming weekend came back to Sarah as she watched the plane lift off. Hayley had insisted on returning to Madison for other homecomings. She'd never invited Sarah to Brown's homecoming, using as an excuse that Sarah had her own bedroom, whereas Hayley shared hers with a roommate. It was as if their romance now had picked up where it left off at college. They were just older, and missing Hayley never got easier. She threw herself into the political arena. Election dates were set six weeks after the recall papers were filed. Three Democratic and six Republican senate seats were up for grabs.

Like any other election, opposing candidates had declared and campaign headquarters had sprung up. Unlike any other election, Republicans found candidates willing to pose as phony Democrats so that primaries would have to be held before the regular elections, slowing down and confusing the process and also making it more expensive. None of the senators up for recall was in Sarah's district, but she could campaign for any of them.

She talked Hayley into coming back the last weekend in June for three days. They stayed at Sarah's apartment, instead of going to the lake. On Saturday they canvassed, walking door to door, reminding the party faithful of the election date and suggesting that they vote early. Lighthearted and happy on Friday, Sarah turned somber and quiet on Sunday. She always told herself she was going to deal with their separation realistically, enjoying Hayley when she could, not letting her unhappiness with the situation spoil their time together, but toward the end of Hayley's visits she struggled to hide the bitterness that threatened to surface.

This, however, was the weekend before the family vacation. Her sister, Beth, along with her baby and husband, and her brother, Jeff, would be at the lake for the Fourth of July week. She welcomed the distraction they would provide. She'd see Hayley off on Sunday and meet Jeff on Friday.

Jeff, who lived in Florida, flew into Outagamie Airport on the first day of July. He rode with her to the lake. Tan and fit, he talked about his fishing charter business before asking, "Do you ever see Hayley or Mike or Eddie?"

"Eddie is still smoking dope and getting drunk. Hayley has been here multiple times because of the protests. I haven't seen Mike, though."

"Maybe they'll be at the lake, and we can get together."

"Eddie's dad sold their cottage. Hayley never comes home. I don't know about Mike."

"How's Mom? Is she still with that woman?"

She couldn't believe he was asking. "Her name is Pat, and yes, she's still with her. Don't you talk to Mom?"

"Yeah. Once a week, but it's so weird."

"Why are Mom and Pat weirder than Dad and his wife?"

"Older guys always go for the young babes."

"She's not a babe, Jeff. She's our stepmother."

"I never thought my mom would turn into a lesbian."

"Think you might suddenly turn into a gay man?" She looked at him and laughed at his expression of horror. "I'm a lesbian. It could be in the genes," she said, virtually coming out to him. Her heart pounded at the admission. She wondered if she would ever get used to talking about her sexual orientation to someone like Jeff, whom she loved despite his homophobia.

"So Eddie really did see you and Hayley in the act. We had more than one fistfight over that."

It was her turn to be horrified. Her skin prickled unpleasantly. That creep, she thought. How dare he ask to sleep at her apartment? She flushed a deep red and blurted, "When?"

"Those summers when we were kids. He used to spy on you. I thought he was just mouthing off."

She fell into an embarrassed and angry silence. It was just like Eddie to turn out to be a voyeur.

"Hey, it's okay, sis. I probably should have told you, but then Mom got involved with Pat and I didn't know what to do with any of it. I thought you must not like guys."

"But I do like guys," she protested. "I like Hayley's brother more than her sometimes. Mike got me through the tree shearing seasons."

"I'm glad Mom's happy," he said, sounding doubtful. "I'm not sure about Dad and what's-her-name."

"Her name is Nancy. What makes you say that?"

"Well, Dad booked a week's charter for himself. She's not coming."

"Maybe she doesn't like to fish. Maybe she gets seasick. There could be a lot of reasons."

"Could be."

When they reached the house, Beth and her little family had already arrived. They were in the kitchen, eating lunch. The baby, Kathryn Paige, banged on the tray of the high chair they'd all used as kids.

"Aww, she is so cute," Sarah said as the dog vied for her attention. She patted him. "Yes, you're cute too, Junior."

"Katydid," Jeff said, giving the baby a nickname.

There followed a round of hugs, voices rising and falling in greetings. Beth put the baby on her feet and she fell on her rump. She climbed her mother's leg and grabbed the dog's scruff and hung on.

"Junior is going to teach her to walk," Beth said, cooing, "What a good dog!" and Junior wagged his tail while they all laughed.

"Are you hungry?" Kate asked.

"Of course. It's lunchtime," Jeff said. He gave his mom a big hug, and Sarah remembered what a mama's boy he'd been. No wonder he worried when he thought his mother liked women better than men.

After lunch, they all went down to the beach. Beth's husband, Cory, carried his daughter. At the water's edge, Beth took the baby and sat her in the water. She tried to grab a wavelet and looked at her hand in surprise when it held nothing. She managed to get a handful of sand and tried to taste it before her dad opened her fist, then picked her up again and walked out into the lake.

The days went by too quickly. Sarah found herself counting them down, not because she wanted time to hurry by, but because she wanted it to slow down. She was finding this a vacation to cherish.

They played volleyball while the baby slept, enlisting Callie Callahan and Vicki Browning from down the beach. They skied behind Vicki's speedboat. Sarah and Beth and Kate read, while Jeff and Cory fished or threw things for the dog to retrieve or volleyed a ball across the net. They ate fabulous meals and played cards on the porch after dark. Through it all, Sarah seethed silently against Eddie.

When it was over and Sarah drove Jeff to the airport, she thought to herself that it seemed as if she was always taking someone to the airport. It was never herself.

***

On July 19, she watched the results of the first recall election at the campaign headquarters of one of the Democratic senators who had fled the state to slow down passage of the Budget Repair

Bill. A low buzz of talk filled the room. No Republican had posed as a Democrat for this recall election, so there had been no primary. Stretched out in an uncomfortable folding chair, she had her gaze fixed on the TV monitor with the results running across the bottom of the screen when someone said, "Hey, where did you come from?"

She looked up into eyes as green as Hayley's and jumped to her feet. "Mike!" Although she knew he worked in Green Bay, she hadn't seen him since the summer after graduation. "So you're involved too. Hayley said you're an engineer for the DOT."

"Of course, I'm involved. First there were the furloughs. Now the extra costs for benefits and insurance. Haven't had a raise in years." He smiled wryly. The lights caught the coppery colors in his thick hair.

"Why not go into the private sector?"

"A lot of us worked during furlough days for nothing. I know it sounds egotistic, but we perform a public service. Makes you feel useful, if unappreciated. You're a teacher, right?"

"I am."

He nodded. "They did renew your contract."

"For a year. A lot of teachers retired anyway."

They looked at each other in silence for the space of a moment. "Have you seen Hayley?"

"A few times, during the protests."

"I keep in touch with her through her blog. We had a falling out about her almost never coming home. Mom and Dad miss her." He rocked back on his heels before asking, "Did you hear? Eddie is working for the law firm doing the redistricting?"

"Yeah, he told me," she said. A flush heated up her skin as she wondered if Eddie had also told him about spying on her and Hayley.

"Remember your first year shearing Christmas trees, the first week when everyone was betting on you quitting. Why didn't you?" he asked with a grin, dragging a chair near her.

"A matter of pride, I guess. If a scrawny kid like you could do it, so could I."

"I think of shearing trees whenever I want to quit, whenever I think something is hopeless. I measure everything against that unbearable first week when I thought my arms were going to fall off and the flies and mosquitoes were driving me mad and the sun was beating me into the sand, and I know I can get through anything."

The measuring part had never occurred to her. "Three summers of torment. I thought I was some kind of superwoman."

"You were."

"I never could keep up with you," she said fondly.

The senator walked over to them, and they stood up to shake hands. "Hi, Mike." He looked at her and smiled.

"This is Sarah Sweeney, my fellow tree shearer and childhood friend." Mike winked at her.

"I've been working in the Kaukauna office. It's closer to home. Going out of state like you all did to slow down the Budget Repair Bill was brilliant."

"Well, thanks. It was a last-ditch effort at compromise." His smile broadened and he turned to Mike. "Wish you were on my staff, Mike. I could use someone with your organizing skills."

"I'll think about it, but I'm an engineer and our road building policies need to be reorganized too. Since we're so short of cash, we should be maintaining what we have, not building more four-lane highways."

Senator Hansen nodded, his attention diverted by a heavyset young man. "Excuse me," he said and thanked them both again before moving off to another group.

When victory was declared his, she left, walking out the door with Mike. As they separated to go to their respective vehicles, he said, "Say hello to Hayley for me if you talk to her."

She drove home, elated with the Democratic win, ignoring her vibrating cell phone till she locked her apartment door behind her and listened to the voice mail from Hayley. "Congratulations on the first win. Call me in the morning."

***

"I saw your brother last night. He said to say hello."

"Hello back."

"Why haven't you met up with him when you've been here?"

"He'd just nag me about going home to see Mom and Dad. I

can either see you or Mom and Dad. Which would you rather?" Her tone was sharp.

"Can't we do both?"

"Maybe next time."

"He reads your blog."

"Mike's the good son. I'm the reprobate."

"Why do you think that, Hayley?"

"I didn't call to talk about this."

"Did you find another place to live?" Something else Hayley probably didn't want to discuss, she thought.

"Not yet. The newspaper is folding. It's breaking my heart, Sarah. I loved that little rag."

"Maybe you can freelance." Maybe she would come home.

"A lot of reporters are freelancing. Too many." She changed the subject. "What are you going to do today?"

"Make phone calls for the August ninth election. I'm going to see Mom on Friday, though, and maybe stay the rest of the month. I can make calls from there. Why don't you come home?"

"I'm broke."

"I'll send money for a ticket. You're always paying to come see me."

"I'll think about it."

"Don't just think about it. Check the fares and call me."

"Where do we stay? With your mom or mine? Call me when you've figured that out."

She flipped her phone shut. She hadn't thought about where they would stay when they were at the lake. How could Hayley not stay with her own family? Sarah had never spent the night at Hayley's house. No one would understand, nor would they get it if Hayley slept at Sarah's place instead of her own. That was okay when they were kids, but not now. They'd be sneaking away looking for places to make love.

It was only then that she remembered she hadn't told Hayley about Eddie spying on them and then ratting about it.

***

It was the kind of day she loved—hot and windy. She quickly

changed into her swimsuit and walked down to the beach, savoring the smell of the pines and the sight of the restless lake. Her mom sat in a beach chair in the shade of the boathouse, her head bent to a book. Junior gave her arrival away, running with a joyous bark to ram his nose in her crotch.

"Yes, I love you too. Sit." The dog sat and she stroked his silken ears while he whined his pleasure deep in his throat.

Her mother turned to greet her. "You're here!" She offered Sarah a big smile, her eyes hidden behind dark glasses, and Sarah hoped she would look as good when she reached her age. "How are you, sweetie?" she asked, hugging Sarah against her.

She'd been here a little over a week ago and yet it seemed longer. "Where's Pat?" Pat had been at the lake only for the Fourth of July weekend during the family vacation.

"In Oshkosh, staying with a friend, working to get Jessica King elected. So, you're taking a break?"

"Yes. I couldn't stay away." She was always drawn to the lake in summer, maybe because the season was so short. "I can make phone calls from here. I use my cell anyway. We all do." She was thinking that Pat could do the same, unless she was canvassing or helping run the office.

"Well, I'm glad you're here. It was kind of lonely after you kids left."

She dumped her towel and book in the chair next to her mother's. "Want to go for a swim?"

"Sure."

They waded in up to their necks, where they swayed on tiptoes until they were lifted off their feet. The lake was relatively quiet with only one speedboat buzzing around. She thought of Eddie and felt a flush of anger. The thought of confronting him made her cringe.

"How is Hayley?"

"I saw Mike Tuesday night at Green Bay's Democratic headquarters. He looked good, but he and Hayley don't see much of each other. She doesn't come home much for some reason."

"Maybe if you asked her, she would."

She wished she could see her mother's eyes. "I did ask her. She's broke. I offered to send her money for the fare."

"That was generous of you."

"Well, it costs her to come to Madison and the Fox Cities."

"Have you been to see her?"

"No." How to explain Kristina? "Her roommate doesn't want me there."

"I'm sorry."

Sarah looked away. Her heart was thudding in her throat, leaving her feeling a little frantic. She swam off a ways on her back and stared at the blue, blue sky while wondering how to talk to her mother about Hayley. It was Brook she had poured her heart out to at the university, and then she had bottled it all up again. Right now it seemed hopeless, and she was filled with despair and an almost unbearable longing.

"How did you feel about Pat when you met her?" she dared to ask.

"Comfortable."

"Well, I don't exactly feel comfortable," Sarah said, wondering if they were on the same page, the one they'd never discussed. "I mean, she left me and she's not coming back, not to stay, and I can't go there."

"It must hurt terribly."

"Remember that summer after I graduated from college, Mom? Did you know I was even around?"

"I was so worried about Gordie. I don't think I've ever been so scared—afraid that madman would kill one of us—and I didn't know how to keep you safe except by sending you away."

"But did you notice that Hayley wasn't around?" She spit out a stream of water.

"Yes. I should have said something. I knew even then there was something special between you and Hayley, but I was too busy worrying about everyone's safety to think how you must have felt."

"She dropped me, Mom, just like that. She didn't write or call or come home to explain. I didn't know what to do without her. I didn't know someone could take such a chunk out of your life." She kicked harder as if to drive away her demons and put distance between herself and her mother.

"I'm sorry, sweetie. I know. What I don't know is what makes anyone love someone so much that life without that person seems empty."

There was a silence while Sarah digested this information and the fact that she and her mom were actually talking about how she felt about Hayley.

"So why is Pat gone?"

"The recalls are important to her."

"Really, Mom?" she said.

"I only know that she feels as if what she's doing is important, Sarah. She's staying with a very dear friend, and you and I are finally talking about Hayley, which wouldn't have happened if she were here. Would it? So something good has come about because she's not here."

Her mother was right, of course. Had Pat been there they wouldn't be talking about Hayley except in the most casual way. "Mom, do you ever feel like something is wrong with you?"

"Because of Pat? I worried about how you kids would react, especially Jeff. I seldom talk about it. It doesn't come up in conversation, but it feels so natural when Pat and I are together."

Sarah was thinking about what Jeff had said about their mother, how he obviously had never accepted Pat as her mom's partner, but then he apparently felt the same way about her dad's wife. She swam toward shore and followed her mother out of the water.

CHAPTER TEN

Summer 2011

When she left the lake on the first Sunday in August, Pat still hadn't returned home. She'd called every day. Sarah witnessed those calls but never heard even one side of the conversation, because her mom always walked away. She hated leaving, but she had signed up to canvass. Six Republicans were up for recall on August 9. Her cell rang on the way home and she answered without glancing at the display.

"Hey, it's me," Hayley said. "Can you pick me up at the airport at eleven fifteen tomorrow morning? I'm coming in on Delta."

Her body responded as it always did to Hayley's voice. It came alive. "I'm heading back from the lake right now."

"Good."

"I didn't know you were coming."

"We'll talk about it when I get there. Okay? I've got a lot of stuff to do between now and then."

Dazed with joy, she sat in her car outside her apartment building, hardly remembering the drive home. Her energy level, which had plummeted when she left the lake, had rebounded. Inside, she channeled her restlessness into a cleaning frenzy—picking up and vacuuming and dusting and wiping down the counters and stove—before making a list and going to the store. It would all be wasted on Hayley, who never seemed to care whether a place was clean or cluttered.

As she watched Hayley walk toward the gate the next morning, she was struck by her disheveled appearance. Her rumpled clothes and messy ponytail were disturbing enough, but her lack of expression, her evident listlessness was alarming.

"I have luggage this time," Hayley gave Sarah the briefest of hugs. No smile. No kiss. "Lots of it."

As they waited by the carousel for the baggage to appear, Sarah asked, "Are you planning to stay a while?"

"Yep. Forever. Isn't that what you want?"

"Only if you do," Sarah said, warned by Hayley's tone to pick her words carefully. What she didn't want was a fight.

"Well, you keep asking. So here I am, prepared to move in with you."

Sarah shot a nervous glance at the people around them. She hated scenes, and they were attracting attention. Just then the carousel belt jerked into motion and the first bag appeared.

A blinding sun poured down on them as they rolled Hayley's four large suitcases out to Sarah's car. They stuffed two in the hatchback and two in the backseat before climbing into the front.

"This is a nice surprise," Sarah said to break the silence that had fallen between them.

"Is it? The end of my career is a nice surprise?" Hayley snorted.

"Can't you blog anywhere?" she said softly, her heart beating an anxious tattoo against her ribs, her happiness turned to wariness.

"You have to have something to blog about. Small town USA doesn't resonate everywhere, especially on the coasts."

She started the engine. "Oh, Hayley, that is so snobby. What the hell happened?"

"I spent my last dollar to get here, and last night I slept at the airport. I'll probably end up moving back in with my parents." She said it like there could be no worse fate.

"I thought you were moving in with me." Sarah kept her eyes on the road as they turned onto Spencer Street. She had only seen Hayley like this once, when Sarah had left the lake to begin her senior year at college. Perhaps Hayley knew then she wouldn't be coming back.

"We'll see how that works out."

"Is living with me the worse scenario you can imagine?" She was getting a little irate.

"Use your imagination, Sweeney. If you had to go live with me or your mom and Pat or your dad and his wife because you couldn't support yourself, how would you feel?"

"That could happen," Sarah said as she parked in front of the apartment building. "I may be out of a job next year."

"Great." Hayley got out of the car and pulled the two bags out of the backseat. "We can be homeless together."

Sarah dragged the other two out of the car and wheeled them inside. "I'm starving," she said, standing the bags on end in the living area. "How about a sandwich?"

They sat at the table next to the sliding doors that looked out onto a patio. Sarah's apartment was just down the road from a nature preserve and a few blocks from Lake Winnebago. Hayley downed the sandwich quickly.

"So, what were you going to do today?"

"Go to headquarters and make some calls. Why don't we go to the nature preserve instead and then to High Cliff and swim?"

"How was your mom?"

"Alone." And to divert attention from her mom being alone, she said, "Did you know that Eddie used to find our hiding places and spy on us?"

Hayley's head shot up. "How do you know that?"

"Jeff told me when he was here. He said they had some fistfights over that. Eddie probably told Mike too."

"That bastard," Hayley said heatedly, and then she laughed. "He probably beat off while watching."

"I don't think that's funny, Hayley. It makes me feel slimy."

Hayley laughed harder. "Wouldn't you have watched? I would."

"Would you have told everybody? Would you have asked if they wanted to watch too? And then have the nerve to show up at my apartment?" She was incensed all over again.

Hayley said, "Sarah, you're way too serious."

"Yeah well, if you're okay with some creep watching us fuck, you're not serious enough. And what if he shows up again?"

"Just pretend it never happened. Eddie is an opportunist. He's also without scruples. Maybe the two go together. He's generous too. Who hauled us around the lake in his boat? Who shared the beer and marijuana?"

"Who is helping to redistrict?"

"He's probably apolitical."

"And that makes it okay?"

Hayley shrugged. "He is without malice. To him it's no doubt just a job."

They walked the boardwalks at the nature preserve and went through the beautiful building. After, they drove to High Cliff State Park and made their way across the grass to the beach. There they dropped their towels near the water, piling their shorts and T-shirts on top, and waded into Lake Winnebago. A couple of boats were anchored offshore. A few swimmers stood in the water. A few more lay on the beach. Mothers watched their little kids as they splashed near shore.

A few feet out the sandbars began. The Wolf and Fox rivers were the main tributaries to this 137,700-acre lake. The Fox River drained Lake Winnebago into Green Bay. Winnebago was an Indian word for smelly waters. It referred to the fishy odor it had had before the Fox River was dammed, which raised the lake's depth by three feet. It was still a shallow lake, only twenty feet at its deepest, and a dangerous body of water in a storm.

They walked over the sandbars into deeper and deeper water till they were swimming. The afternoon was getting away from them, Sarah noted by the height of the sun. They could go to campaign headquarters tomorrow.

Hayley asked, "Why was your mom alone?"

"Pat is in Oshkosh, working at Jessica King's headquarters and staying with a friend." Sarah hoped the "dear" friend was nothing more than that.

"Think I still have a chance with her?" Hayley said and burst into laughter at Sarah's glare and splash of water. "It's so easy to get to you. You've got to lighten up."

"Like you were light when I picked you up at the airport?"

"Sorry about that. My life crashed. It's hard to be sunny about failure."

"Don't talk like that, Hayley. You've got this great blog." She read it every day.

"Yeah well, I'm going to have to find another job."

"I'd love to live with you, Hayley."

"You might change your mind after a few days."

All Sarah had wanted was to wake up and go to sleep with Hayley. She hadn't thought how it would feel if it wasn't what Hayley wanted.

In bed that night, Hayley immediately fell asleep. "Sorry. I can't get it up," were her last words.

"I thought that was one of the good things about being a woman. You didn't have to get it up." But she was talking to herself. She read till the book, *Sarah's Key*, fell on her nose as she drifted off. Her mother always said everything looked better in the morning. She turned off the lamp, desperately hoping that would be the case this time.

***

"Do we have to go?" Hayley grumbled at breakfast.

"Well, I do. You can stay here." Sarah said from the stove where she was making oatmeal.

"What will I do here?"

"Work on your blog?"

"Tell the world what failure is like." With chin in hand, Hayley slumped over the table.

"I think you'd find plenty of sympathizers. People always like to know there are others as unhappy as they are," she said and held her breath, hoping Hayley would say she wasn't unhappy, at least not with her, but she said nothing.

"I'll be home midafternoon. I'll probably stop at the store. Any suggestions for dinner?" She filled two bowls and set them on the table.

Hayley heaped brown sugar on her oatmeal and folded it over and over with her spoon.

"You used to like oatmeal," Sarah said, watching with growing annoyance, wondering why she'd bothered to make it. They could have had toast or dry cereal.

"I do." She took a bite before stirring it again.

Sarah suddenly couldn't wait to leave. She ate quickly and put her bowl in the dishwasher. After brushing her teeth, she grabbed her wallet and her keys. "See you in a few."

Hayley met her eyes. "Have a good time."

Like making phone calls was a good time, she thought. "Call me if you change your mind about coming." Never in all the years she'd known Hayley had she wanted to get away from her. If she stayed any longer, she was afraid she'd burst into tears and that was something she absolutely didn't want to do.

Give her a chance, she reasoned once she was in the car. How would it feel if she lost her job? Fortunately, they'd signed the contract the night before Walker's budget passed. If Hayley made the blog work, she'd be all right. Sarah thought the blog was good—interesting, worth reading—but of course she was biased.

There were three people at campaign headquarters, two women on the phones and another at the front table. The dreariness of the office hit her—its scattering of empty tables and chairs, the cheap paneled walls and tiled floor.

***

When they were getting ready for bed that night, Sarah turned her back to undress, not something she would normally do, but she felt so vulnerable.

Hayley's hands slid around her and cupped her breasts. "Don't hide yourself from me."

She shivered and leaned back. The tears she had been fighting started to escape.

"I should have warmed my hands first."

When Sarah's arms dropped to her sides in a defenseless motion, Hayley tightened her grip and buried her face in Sarah's neck. Sarah placed her head against Hayley's and wept— not sure why she was crying, but unable to stop.

"Don't," Hayley said in a choked voice.

She turned and pressed herself against Hayley's T-shirt, the one with the skyscrapers that read *NYC—The Sky's the Limit*. Never before had she seen Hayley cry, not even when they had separated at the end of summer. She felt wetness on Hayley's cheeks when they kissed and wondered if passion was always greater when the relationship was threatened. Did it signal the beginning of the end?

By the time they made it to the bed they were naked and slippery with sweat. Sarah's mouth felt bruised, and Hayley's hands moved over her roughly as if she were angry. For some reason this excited Sarah even more, and she responded in kind.

When they fell apart, the sheets under them soaked, Sarah thought she could see the future and it looked grim—one of jealousy and mistrust and more of this desperate passion.

Hayley was smiling, though, as if the sun had broken through. Sarah's heart lifted a little. "Did you like that?"

"Well, it was different." Sort of like a battle between love and resentment. "We made a mess of the sheets."

"That's all you can say?" Hayley's eyes were dark with only a thin line of green around the pupils. She reached up and turned on the fan over the bed. "I'm about to boil over."

"Me too." She watched the blades whip around, their shadows elongated by a streetlight.

***

Sarah resorted to nagging the morning they were to leave for the lake. She wanted to get going, and Hayley was dragging her behind. First, they made long drawn-out love. Whenever Sarah tried to hurry it up with hands or mouth, Hayley pulled back. "Make it last," she whispered.

This was another first for Sarah. She had always tried to prolong sex with Hayley, but she was anxious to be on the road before Hayley changed her mind about going. That was more important to her than rutting around in bed for an hour. They could do this any time, she thought as Hayley began a long slow journey down Sarah's length with her tongue. This was how they usually ended up, so the finale was in sight.

They still had to shower and eat. Today it would be cereal or toast, something quick. They also had to pack but only enough for a day and a night. Hayley had been living out of her suitcases. This was Sarah's last thought before sensation took over. When she heard someone cry out, she wasn't sure if it was herself or Hayley or both of them.

"We might not be doing this for a while," Hayley said as she crawled up the tangled sheets and collapsed next to Sarah.

Sarah leaped out of bed. "Want to save water and shower with me?"

"If you put it that way, I guess so," Hayley said with a smile, and Sarah relaxed a little. Women who catered to their men had always annoyed her. Now she understood this behavior. She was tiptoeing around Hayley's moods.

The trip to the lake usually took a little over an hour. Hayley had wanted to drive and they were whizzing west on Highway 10 at eighty miles per hour. Sarah leaned back in the passenger seat, trying to ignore the speed. If they got cited, though, she'd probably be the one to pay since Hayley was broke.

"Maybe you should slow down a little," she said as Hayley pulled into the passing lane, leaving someone else breathing their exhaust. "Why are we in such a hurry?" She recalled her mom asking her the same question and wondered if she was going to turn into her mother.

Hayley grinned at her. "I guess you've never ridden with me, have you?"

She'd heard stories about Hayley's driving. Around the campfire, her brother had joked about her missing curves at night because she was going so fast. Once she'd ended up in a swamp. A farm tractor had pulled the vehicle out. Her dad had taken the car away from her for a month.

When they turned off onto State Road 49, Sarah gave up. She squeezed her eyes shut when two deer bounded across County Road A and Hayley slammed on the brakes. Almost everyone who lived in these parts had hit at least one deer. What would they do if it was still alive? They couldn't leave it thrashing next to the road. Was that the difference between them? She erred on the side of caution, and Hayley was a risktaker. Did that make them incompatible or did it balance them out?

"I want to stop and say hey to your mom. Okay?" Hayley said as she turned into Sarah's driveway, passing her childhood home on the way.

"Sure. You can take the car to your place." She wouldn't need it till she left, and once she got to her mom's she knew she wouldn't want to go anywhere else. Besides, Hayley had taken one of her large suitcases rather than repack.

They walked through the kitchen and main room to the porch, where beyond the trees they saw Sarah's mom on the beach, reading. Halfway down the steps to the lake, Junior leaped up from the shade of the boathouse and with a deep "Woof" ran toward them. The dog danced around her before putting his huge feet on her chest, leaving sandy footprints. "Down!" she ordered, struggling to maintain her balance.

He sat in front of her, his tail brushing the sandy ground, his tongue hanging out—a picture of doggy joy. Her mom was standing, grinning at them. She called the dog to her side and waited.

When Hayley threw her arms around Kate, Sarah wanted her to go hug her own mother. She stood on the hot sand, feeling the pull of the water, her eyes on the restless lake. It bothered her that Hayley seemed to prefer her mother to her own. Why she cared she didn't know.

"I'm going to put my suit on. Say hello to your mom, Hayley." It was a hint for Hayley to leave. "Bring the car back whenever."

From her bedroom windows she watched Hayley talking to her mom. When she gave her mom another hug and headed up the stairs, Sarah breathed a sigh of relief. As soon as she heard the car door slam and the engine start, she went downstairs.

Her mother was standing in the kitchen with the dog. Her eyes searched Sarah's. "Too bad Hayley lost her job."

"Did she tell you that she doesn't want to be here?"

Her mom nodded. "I don't think it's personal, Sarah."

"Mom, why isn't Pat home?"

"The election is Tuesday. She just feels she has to be there to make a difference."

"Don't you?"

"I can make phone calls from here, and there is the dog. What would I do with him if I went to Oshkosh? How long can you stay?"

"I thought I'd go back tomorrow. It was the only way to get Hayley here. She almost never comes home, Mike said."

"Would you like something to eat?"

Sarah glanced at the large clock on the wall. It was already after eleven. "Not yet." She filled her water bottle, grabbed a beach towel out of the closet, her suntan lotion and book. "Let's go swimming."

The water closed over her. The dog had raced her to the end of the pier and launched himself into the air as she did. She swam underwater several feet, distancing herself from the animal, before surfacing.

"Ha, fooled you," she said as Junior redoubled his efforts to reach her. He swam circles around whoever was in the water as if worried about their safety. She floated on her back, cradled by the buoyant water, her gaze fixed on the blue sky.

Her mom called Junior to shore, giving Sarah space to enjoy herself. She was still out there when Hayley arrived minutes later. She broke the surface near Sarah.

"Did you even have time to say hello?" Sarah asked.

"Yeah. Mom was so surprised to see me and so happy. She cried. I think I'm going to stay for a few days and do the family thing. I brought the car back."

"Okay," she said, not sure whether she was relieved or disappointed. "Let me know when you want me to come get you."

"Sarah, I may try to get my old job back. I can blog from home." Was this "home" now, the place she had been avoiding so long?

It made Sarah want to be here too. She was the one who

loved the area. No matter how gently put, it was a slap in the face. "I thought you hated it here."

"Leaving is different from coming back. It's like seeing the place with new eyes. I don't know how long I'll feel this way. I'll miss the city lights. I know I'll miss you."

"But you don't have to miss me."

"You're the one who has been trying to get me to come home and spend time with my family."

They were treading water, going nowhere. She was suddenly very tired, very sad. She thought of the huge suitcase in the back of her car, sure Hayley had put it in just in case she decided to stay.

"It will give you a reason to come back here."

"I don't need a reason. I'm the one who loves it here." Maybe she'd stay through Tuesday and watch the election returns with her mom.

As they waded toward shore, Sarah battled with herself. She'd be going back to an empty apartment, one with echoes of Hayley in it. She wasn't sure she could handle that. There was another recall election the next week, but it was for two candidates up north.

"You don't have to go home, do you? When does school start?" Hayley asked. Droplets of water clung to her golden skin, and Sarah looked at her with longing.

"After Labor Day weekend."

"Hey, it would be like old times. I'll come back later for another swim. I'm going home and call Jenkins. Keep your fingers crossed."

Fingers crossed? Going home? Sarah stood dumbfounded as Hayley said goodbye to Kate and bounded up the steps. She was stunned. A few days of separation had turned into something permanent.

She wrapped herself in a beach towel and plunked down in the chair next to her mother. The dog put his large head in her lap as if he sensed something wrong. "Did you hear that, Mom? She wants her old job at the gas station back."

"Well, jobs are hard to come by. Maybe she needs the money. At least she won't be a thousand miles away."

She supposed that was a plus. She could see her anytime. It was disturbing to realize how little she really knew about Hayley.

Never would she have predicted this turn of events. "What?" Her mother had said something.

"What would you do if you lost your job, Sarah?"

"I'd have to come home, but she didn't have to. She could have stayed with me." Hayley had never talked to her about moving back in her childhood home, but Sarah was sure she'd been thinking about it or she wouldn't have taken the suitcase.

"Would you want to live with Hayley if you had no job and no money?"

She glanced at her mom, who had spent over twenty years writing an advice column. "What's your advice, Mom?"

"Serious?" Her mother took her sunglasses off and looked Sarah in the eyes.

Apparently she had never asked for advice. "Yes, I'm serious."

"Give her time to get her feet under her. She may be floundering. If you define yourself by your job, losing it is like losing your identity."

"Why would she want to be defined by working for Jenkins?"

"This is probably an interim job. Anyway, she doesn't have it yet, does she?"

"She wouldn't even go home for a visit, and now she wants to stay. I don't understand."

"People are complex. I don't think we know what we'd do under certain circumstances. This may be one of those times."

Around midnight long after she and her mom had gone to bed, when she was still flopping around unable to sleep, she heard someone on the stairs. She froze, her gaze fixed on the door. Her eyes had adjusted to the dark, and she saw the knob turn. Her heart beat wildly as she thought about where to hide. Under the bed?

"Hey, it's me," a soft voice said, and she exhaled.

"And I thought you were going to rape me or worse."

"I am. Move over." And they were back in Sarah's single bed as if they were kids again.

"Not very roomy," Sarah said. It seemed as if they fit better when they were younger.

"I couldn't sleep knowing you were so close, but I have to be at Jenkins's by seven, and Mom doesn't know I'm gone. I'll have to leave after the deed."

Instead, they fell asleep in each other's arms, and Sarah woke up to an empty bed. Light flooded the room. It almost seemed as if last night hadn't happened, except she vaguely remembered Hayley leaving. She had been unable to hold onto her.

At noon, Hayley called to say she'd be over for a swim after work. She spoke in a low voice. "It's weird being back here."

"I'll bet. Will I see you at midnight again?" She had walked away from where she'd been sitting with her mother.

"Maybe I'll just tell Mom I'm going to spend the night at your place, for old times' sake."

"Can't wait," she said, when what she wanted to ask was when were they going to move in together like grown-ups.

CHAPTER ELEVEN

Summer 2011

She left the lake Wednesday morning, not because she wanted to go home but because she thought she should. She had been so sure by the positive responses to phone calls and canvassing that her candidate would win. It had not been the case. The election in the district she had worked was called early with the incumbent the predicted winner. The Democrats had wrested two seats from Republican candidates, closing the gap in the state senate to a one-vote majority for the Republicans.

As the scenery flashed by unnoticed, she wondered how this could have happened. The turnout had been thirty percent in some precincts, unheard of in a nonpresidential election. The Republican legislature had been busy changing the laws, making it more difficult to vote, making it more expensive for the state, since they had to provide free photo IDs for those without driver's licenses. These changes wouldn't go into effect till 2012, though. Voters had received phone calls and mailings with incorrect dates and addresses about when and where to mail absentee ballots. A post office box for a conservative group was given as an official government address for absentee ballots. But these attempts at deception couldn't have fooled many.

When she let herself into her apartment, the place reminded her of a hotel room—airless and lonely. After throwing open the windows and sliding glass doors to the patio, she returned the voice mail from Jane. "We lost," she said with obvious dismay. She'd really thought they would win the three districts they needed for a majority.

"We won two seats. All of those districts were Republican strongholds. If you look at it that way, it was a victory."

"It doesn't feel like a win right now."

"I knew it wouldn't. That's why I called, but it is." There were two more Democratic senators up for recall on August 16. "Margaret and I are going to Minocqua, partly to canvass and partly to vacation. Want to come with us?"

"I'll think about it." But she knew she wouldn't. She'd go back to the lake, if anywhere.

The other voice mail was from Brook. As she returned the call that evening, she was seriously considering going for a visit if Brook brought it up again.

Brook answered on the second ring. "I thought maybe that would be you. Wait a minute. Let me turn down the TV. I don't need to hear all the bad news." The background noise disappeared. "How the hell are you anyway?"

"Kind of down." Why wouldn't she be with Hayley moving back home and the recalls not living up to her expectations?

"Come on out. I'll cheer you up or die trying. Don't you have a couple weeks before school starts?"

"Let me look at the cost and call you back."

"Never mind the cost. I'll send you an e-ticket. I have tons of free miles."

"I can't take your free miles."

"That's what they're for. Start packing. Is Friday all right?"

"That only gives me one day to get ready."

"You can do it."

Excitement made Sarah smile. She laughed a little. "You're nuts."

"We both know that. Wear your hiking boots. Let's shoot for Friday, the twelfth and a return date of August twenty-fifth. That's almost two weeks. Can you do that?"

She looked at her Sierra Club calendar, hanging on the kitchen wall. "My first staff orientation is August twenty-ninth. So yeah." The first day for students was September 7, the day after Labor Day.

"Okay. I am so excited. I'll get back with you."

She emptied her drawers on the bed. She'd need a backpack and another bag. Jeans, shorts, T-shirts, a sweatshirt, one good pair of capris, another pair of shoes and underwear and socks. She'd wear the hiking boots with her zip-off hiking pants, a nice T-shirt and a lightweight jacket.

Brook called back in less than a half hour. "Look at your e-mail and see if those times and dates are okay."

After a moment of panicky doubt, she mentally shook herself. What could happen in two weeks?

"Think of it as a much needed vacation," Brook said. "Getting away will help put things in perspective. You got a lot going on there, roomie."

"Okay. Book it before I change my mind." She doubted that a two-week trip would change anything, though.

"Will do. I can't wait to see you."

"Same here." Brook's offer had come as a breath of fresh air. She'd been drowning. When she came back, she'd have staff orientation and then school would start, and she wouldn't have time to feel so out of sync with everything.

She heard from Hayley around seven thirty. "You didn't call."

"I'm flying to Washington Friday to see Brook. She's been trying to get me to visit. Thought it was a good time with you gone and my part in the recalls over."

Silence. Then, "You didn't tell me you were thinking of going out there."

"Because I hadn't been. You didn't say you were thinking of moving back home."

"I wasn't."

"Then why did you take that big suitcase with you?"

"Is this a tit-for-tat thing?"

"No, Hayley. I haven't seen Brook since graduation. This is just what it seems. A long overdue visit."

"I was thinking about coming to Appleton this weekend to get my other suitcases."

"I won't be here."

"Does your mom have a key?"

"Yes, but can't it wait till I get back?"

"I need some of those things."

"I have to call Mom anyway."

"What time does your flight leave?"

She told her. There would be no chance to see each other beforehand. "Listen, let me call Mom. I'll catch you later. Okay?"

"Call me when you're in bed. We can pretend we're together."

"Cell phones aren't secure, Hayley."

"I miss you already, Sweeney. Promise to call me every day."

"I miss you too." Too much, she thought as she pushed in her mom's number.

"Hey, Mom, it's me."

"Hi, me." Her mother sounded happy.

"Pat must be home," she said.

"Yes, as a matter of fact. The results must have disappointed you, honey, but we won two seats and nearly tied up the senate."

"I know, Mom. I just feel bummed." She told her mother about her travel plans and that Hayley would be stopping by for a key.

"But that's wonderful, sweetie. I'm so glad you're getting away. Pat wants to talk to you."

"Hey, congratulations," she said with as much enthusiasm as she could muster. The candidate Pat had worked to elect had won, but not by as many votes as Sarah had expected. The loser was the one cheating on his wife.

"We almost did it."

"The phone calls and canvassing fooled me."

"That's because you were talking to the base. There were no

polls, but all the districts were solid Republican districts, except maybe one."

"I thought Clark would win too."

"A lot of TV advertising against him."

"Yeah and he said some things he shouldn't have."

"Well, your mom's proud of you. So am I. You worked hard."

"So did you." At least they were on the same side politically. She wasn't sure where her dad and his wife stood, which made her realize that it had been weeks since she'd talked to him. For some reason, an image of her dancing with her dad came to mind, and she felt a physical pain, a tightening of her chest. She missed the dad she had once known.

Pat put her mom back on and Sarah talked to her a few more minutes, saying she'd call when she got to Washington.

Around ten as she lay in bed, she phoned Hayley and left a message. "Wish I could sleep like you do, Hayley. I'll call you sometime tomorrow. Love you."

Hayley woke her at six. "Sorry I fell asleep last night. We were crazy busy yesterday."

She stretched, spreading her toes and yawning. "Hey, you're here now. I needed to wake up anyway. I've got a lot to do before I get on that plane." Just saying she was getting on a plane made it more real, more exciting. The last time she'd flown it was to Florida with family to visit her dad's parents.

"Wish I were going with you."

"Wish you were too," she lied.

"No, you don't."

"Maybe not. I think I need some time away."

"Away from me?"

"It's you who moved home, not me. Let's not do this. Okay?"

"You're angry."

"Well, yeah. Wouldn't you be?"

"I don't know. Maybe. I had no plans when I went home except to touch base with my family. Mike is coming this weekend."

She didn't believe the bit about having no plans. "Say hello to him for me."

***

When she landed at SeaTac, she followed everyone else down the escalator and boarded the train for the main terminal. She was to meet Brook at the baggage pickup. No one without a ticket could get through the gates to the concourses or the satellites where boarding took place.

She looked around for Brook when she reached the lower level. Some of the people standing around the carousel she recognized from her plane, and she dropped her backpack to the floor. When she felt a tap on her shoulder, she whirled.

"Hey," Brook said, throwing her arms around Sarah.

"Hey, yourself." She leaned back, grinning at Brook like a fool. "You don't look ten years older." Brook was still a little chunky, but she had the same beautiful skin and ironic smile. One eyebrow arched, and Sarah laughed. "I don't see any wrinkles. I'd know you anywhere."

"You don't get wrinkles out here. Not enough sunshine." Baggage began kicking out of the top of the carousel, and they turned toward the moving belt. "What are we looking for?"

"A small red suitcase with a pink ribbon."

The parking garage was across a walkway. Sarah looked down at the vehicles pulling up and leaving the main terminal. She could hardly believe she was here. She tossed her red suitcase in the back of Brook's Honda Accord.

They sped north on Interstate 5 toward Kirkland, and Brook peppered her with questions about the recalls, interrupting only to point out the floating bridges and the Space Needle. Sarah marveled at the sight of Mount Rainier floating above the skyline of Seattle under a clear sky—like a mirage.

"This is one of the lucky days when Mount Rainier isn't hiding behind clouds. How is it going with you and Hayley?"

Briefly, she recounted Hayley losing the newspaper job she'd loved. How she'd arrived broke and was now back home working her old job at Jenkins Gas and Sport Center. "That was a slap in my face."

"Was it?" Brook chanced a look at her and nearly rear-ended the car in front of them. "I was kind of glad to see Rex go. Now I'm free to do my thing. We're going on a trip, roomie."

Sarah grabbed the dashboard to brace herself. The fast-moving traffic unnerved her. "A trip?" she echoed. "Where?"

"Well, first we'll nose around Redmond. It's a yuppy little town with lots of neat shops. We'll go to the City Market downtown Seattle and watch them throw a few fish around. Tomorrow, we'll drive to Snoqualmie Falls, one of the most frequented tourist stops. It's also Puget Sound's oldest power-generating system. We'll take a trip to Mount St. Helens, because you can't visit Washington and not see the volcano. We'll hike your legs off. What do you say?"

"Sounds wonderful."

"You up to sleeping in a tent? I borrowed an extra sleeping bag and pad."

"You bet."

Brook owned a small condo in a complex on Lake Sammamish. "How lucky can you get," she said as she walked through it—the small living/dining room with fireplace, the separate kitchen, the hallway with stacked washer/dryer behind louvered doors, a first-floor washroom in the foyer. Upstairs were two bedrooms, each with a full-size bath, and an open loft that looked over the living/dining room. Outside the dining room windows and kitchen door at the back was a flower garden with stones for mulch.

"This is lovely, Brook." Sarah would have been green with envy had she not been so pleased for her friend.

"Working for Microsoft helps, and my mom and dad insisted on me living in a safe place, so they pitched in. This is a gated community. Look out the window there toward the far end of the green space. See that tree with white stuff all over it and those tall birds in it and those messy nests?"

"Are they great blue herons?"

"They are. It's a rookery. It smells pretty bad, though. The white stuff is poop. Did you know birds don't pee? Any liquid comes out in their poop."

"Yeah, I think I've heard that or read it."

She had her own bedroom, where she changed out of her hiking pants and boots into capris, a short sleeve pullover and sandals. "Ta-da," she said, coming out to see Brook in a low cut blouse that showed cleavage and hung over her capris. She looked sort of shapeless, like she was pregnant, but that was the style.

"Ready to see Redmond? We'll eat at a Thai restaurant. We have some good ones. Do you like Thai food?"

"Love it." Actually, she was seldom picky and always hungry, yet she somehow stayed skinny.

They parked in downtown Redmond and hit the interesting shops, where she mulled over gifts for her mom and Pat and Hayley and came away with nothing. They ended up at REI, an outdoor gear and camping store, where Brook spent a lot of time looking at the inventory before settling on a pair of hiking socks. After, they walked out on a pier over Lake Sammamish.

"What do you think so far? Want to move into my spare bedroom?" Brook asked.

"Lots of traffic. Lots of people."

"Lots of water and mountains. A plethora of environmentalists."

"You're breaking my heart," Sarah said. "But I can't bear to see my home go from a progressive state to a Mississippi wannabe and do nothing."

"Give up the fight and come where green really is considered gold."

"I can't." She gave Brook a pleading look. "Thanks for asking, though."

"Ready for dinner?" Brook paused outside a restaurant.

"We're kind of young to eat with the early birds," she joked, referring to the elderly.

"Today we will join their ranks."

"Whatever happened to Chandler?" she asked, dipping a vegetable roll in sweet and sour sauce. "Mmm. This is so good."

"I'll give you her e-mail address. You can get in touch with her if you want. She works at Microsoft too and lives with another woman. We roomed together when she first moved out here. Neither of us had a pot to piss in. We have lunch together once in a while at one of the restaurants in the Microsoft complex."

"You never mentioned..."

"I know. I grew less enamored with her the better I knew her. She'll do anything to get ahead and has been really successful within the company. Did you want to see her? Because I could set something up."

"No, Brook. I want to stick to your plans. Chandler filled in when Hayley wasn't around. I know that's kind of mean, but I think she knew it."

That night they packed the camping equipment and loaded the Honda before going to bed. Snoqualmie was a day trip, but Brook wanted to be prepared in case they decided to overnight somewhere.

The next day Sarah stood on the observation deck, galvanized by the water thundering two hundred sixty-eight feet to the Snoqualmie River below. Her legs felt weak as if somehow she might be catapulted into the water that was spraying both her and Brook. The Snoqualmie people once worshipped here, but now Puget Sound Energy owned the land.

The trail descended nine hundred feet to the original powerhouse, which was closed to the public. There was a spectacular view of the falls from this viewpoint, though, and they found a picnic table and ate lunch—peanut butter sandwiches and apples, washed down with water from their bottles.

After, they climbed back up to Salish Lodge and went quickly through the gift shop before heading to Mount Index to see Bridal Veil Falls. The trail dropped into an old logging run. They ended up on a side trail that led to a viewpoint directly below the falls. The hike had seemed short and easy, so when Brook asked if she wanted to climb the steps to Lake Serene, Sarah said, "Of course." She wasn't even winded.

The steps were steep and switched back and forth, crossing streams, climbing another two thousand feet in two miles. She and Brook paused to catch their collective breaths more than once, guzzling from their water bottles. How could stairs be so difficult to navigate?

When they finally reached Lake Serene and sat on "Lunch Rock," they ate the cookies Brook had packed and agreed the scenery was absolutely worth the climb. Adjectives like "magnificent" and "serene" defied descriptions.

At the condo that night, while sitting in Brook's rock garden, enjoying the end of the day with a glass of wine, Sarah felt her cell phone purr in her pocket. She realized she had called neither her mother nor Hayley. She'd actually forgotten about both of them.

"I'm here. We've been climbing mountains," she told Hayley, not mentioning the stairs.

"Out of sight, out of mind, I guess."

"Home seems far away." The fact that Hayley could be jealous too was somehow reassuring.

"I thought maybe you were climbing each other."

"Hey, that's not fair." She glanced at Brook, who got up and moved away. "There's too much distance between us to argue. We can't make up."

"You promised to call."

"I did. I will. How is work?"

Hayley snorted. "Boring. How is Washington?"

"Anything but boring," she said.

"I'm sorry, Sarah. It was a bad day. I undercharged a customer and I have to pay for it. I waited all day for your call, and it didn't come. I really do want you to have a good time or at least not a bad one."

"Thanks," she said wryly, watching Brook pluck dead roses off a bush. She had really wanted Hayley to live with her too. "There's a heron rookery here. Brook has a condo on Lake Sammamish."

"She's done well."

"She works for Microsoft."

"I thought she was going to be a teacher."

"I did too, but she got a master's in business."

"Is she with someone?"

"Not right now."

"I've got to go. Dinner is ready. Can't let it get cold," Haley said with obvious sarcasm.

"What did you do today?"

"Get my stuff out of your apartment."

"So you're really moving in with your parents." It was like a sore tooth. She couldn't leave it alone. Her chest ached.

"I can't just quit my job. I'll be here at least till the end of summer. Then Jenkins might not need me, although he said I'd make a great manager."

"Of course you would. You can do anything." A degree from Brown and she ended up managing a gas station. Keep your mouth shut, she told herself.

"I'll talk to you later."

"Tomorrow," Sarah said. "I'm going to bed early tonight."

They left for Mount St. Helens early the next morning. The day was overcast and drizzly. "Let's hope the sun comes out before we get there, so we can see something," Brook said. "I'm so glad you're here. It gives me a chance to do all these touristy things."

Mount St. Helens was ninety-six miles south of Seattle, Brook noted, as they drove south on Interstate 5. Mount Rainier had disappeared into the clouds, and rain peppered the windshield. "We'll stay overnight if we have to. It's not as amazing as it was the first ten years or so, but it's still a must-see. Around here everyone who was alive in 1980 knows exactly where they were when Mount St. Helens blew."

"Like September 11th, I suppose."

"Or the assassination of JFK for those who lived through it. I heard that somewhere."

More than once, Sarah caught herself gripping the dash. The traffic was stop and go. They were in the car pool lane, which was a little faster. "Is this the way it always is?"

"The roads can't keep up with the increasing population. Everyone wants to live here."

"I'd hoped you'd move to Appleton after graduation. We could have roomed together."

"We still can," Brook pointed out.

"I can't leave. Mom's there, the lake is there, Hayley is there, and I have to stay and try to turn the conservative tide. I know that last part is foolish. How can one person make much difference, but that's how I feel. I want my state back."

Brook patted her hand. "I know. I think you're admirable."

"Well, don't get carried away," she said.

To get to the 110,000-acre Mount St. Helens National Volcanic Monument in the Gifford Pinchot National Forest, they turned onto Spirit Lake Memorial Highway. They were driving through a forest of evergreens when they turned a sharp curve, and Sarah caught her breath.

She had been looking at trees that had been spared the volcano's destructive force. The delineation before and after the curve was sharp and unmistakable. The trees in the valley before her grew among the litter of those felled by the eruption. Although the new forest was thirty years old, the devastation out of which it regenerated itself was still obvious in the litter of logs on the forest floor. She wondered how it must have looked ten years ago or twenty.

"Amazing how the forest has come back after being leveled, isn't it? When I first came out here, it was more dramatic to look at. There are fish in the streams now and new growth everywhere, covering up the devastation. Fifty-seven people were killed, twenty-one were never found, an estimated seven thousand large game animals died along with twelve million salmon and millions of birds and small mammals. Spirit Lake was filled with dead trees and rock debris. The mountain lost some thirteen hundred feet of height. The gases released under pressure blew down or scorched two hundred and thirty square miles of forest. Clouds of ash rose thousands of feet, turning day into night as it drifted downwind, falling over eastern Washington and beyond."

"It's amazing that you remember all that stuff. You're a fountain of information." She was impressed.

"I bring all of my visitors to Mount St. Helens. It's still an active volcano. Let's go to Harmony Viewpoint and hike down to Spirit Lake. It's just a one-mile trail, but it's kind of steep. Wanna?"

"Of course."

"Spirit Lake was created some thirty-five thousand years ago after an eruption and the damming of the Toutle River. When the mountain blew in 1980, nine hundred foot waves swept trees off the surrounding slopes into the lake. Afterward the lake was a mile longer and two hundred feet higher. Logs still cover the surface. It was up till then a remote vacation spot, a getaway."

After hiking down the steep trail, they stood on the shores of the lake and stared over the surface still covered with the mat of logs blown from the hillsides during the 1980 eruption. Sarah thought how impermanent everything was. Harry Truman, the owner and caretaker of Mount St. Helens Lodge, was buried some one hundred fifty feet under the water, as was the resort.

"That is Harmony Falls," Brook said of a small waterfall. "It was five hundred feet high and is now fifty feet tall."

A woman was dispensing information to a group of young people nearby. They clustered around her, staring over the lake. Sarah nudged Brook. "You could do that."

"Don't want to, don't have to." She opened her backpack and took out their lunch. "Hungry?"

"Always." Sarah took an apple. The drizzle had stopped south of Seattle. She turned her face to the sun and stretched her legs. Her phone was turned off. She was only three days into her vacation. She stared at the bowl of the volcano on the other side of the lake. "Can we climb the mountain?"

"It's too late to get a permit. We'll go downtown tomorrow. Eat lunch on the waterfront, take in Pioneer Square and Pike Place Market and the aquarium, and if we can't get all that done in one day, we'll go back the next. We've got plenty of time."

There was also lots of time for talking, and nothing was sacrosanct. Hayley had become a regular topic of conversation. At the aquarium the next day as they watched a sea otter use a rock to crack open a clam or mussel while floating on its back, Brook said, "Maybe she doesn't want to be swallowed up."

"What does that mean?" She didn't have to ask who "she" was.

"Actually, that's how I felt about Ken. I was afraid he and his boring friends would become my life."

"Are you saying I'm boring?"

"No, of course not, but you become a part of someone's life when you commit yourself."

"I thought she and I shared the same interests—the lake, politics." And sex.

At lunch, sitting outside on the waterfront as seagulls screamed overhead, Sarah said, "She thinks I'm way too serious." She took a bite of the grilled salmon salad and continued. "Finding out from my brother of all people that Eddie spied on us made me furious. She thinks I should blow it off. Would you?"

Brook leaned forward, her ample breasts resting on the table. A gull swept low over them, and Brook waved her fist. "Get out of here. They'll snatch the food off your plate or worse. They'll poop on it." She stuffed the rest of her sandwich in her mouth. "I don't know what I'd do, but I wouldn't blow it off. Does your mom know about you and Hayley?"

"She's probably always known. We talked about it once."

Brook leaned further over the table as if to shield it, her gaze on Sarah as if urging her to talk.

"Hayley said she would have watched us too."

"This Eddie sounds creepy."

"I feel that he took something important and made it cheap."

"He was the guy with the speedboat who was always grabbing his crotch?"

Sarah laughed. "Yeah, that's Eddie. He seemed harmless at the time. He was also involved with the GOP's redistricting. He still smokes dope. I don't want to get arrested along with him, but he was once our friend."

"He was never your friend, roomie."

A seagull perched on the back of a vacant chair, and Sarah popped the last bite of salmon in her mouth. "I never had to compete for food with a bird."

"The gray jays are worse. You'll see when we picnic at Mount Rainier."

On the way home, Sarah said, "Ken might have been boringly brilliant, but he was reliable."

"I know. I didn't want reliable. I wanted exciting."

"Well, right now I'd take reliable over exciting. Should I just let her go, Brook?" Could she?

"Not yet." Regular traffic had come to a standstill. They inched forward in the carpool lane. "She's been the one love of your life."

Sarah sighed. "Unfortunately." Her phone was vibrating in her pocket. She fished it out and it stopped. There were many dead areas in the mountains, and she was often cut off in mid-sentence.

At the condo she read an e-mail from Hayley. It said only that she missed her and was already tired of working at Jenkins's. She was writing interest pieces for the local paper.

On the last weekend she and Brook climbed a mountain trail to a small lake. They sat on a tall rock watching a dog retrieve sticks that its owner threw into the icy water. One day was meshing into another. Either they were climbing trails at some mountain, or they were wine tasting at the many wineries around the area. They took the ferry to Whidbey Island on their way to Deception Pass State Park, Washington's most visited spot—according to Brook. They crossed the high bridge over Deception Pass, hiked through old-growth forest and walked the beaches.

On the last night of this last trip they sat around the campfire and ate charred salmon they'd grilled, washing it down with chardonnay from Chateau St. Michelle. They were so comfortable with each other by now that Sarah thought nothing of sharing the most confidential of confidences.

"Maybe it was the sex. Do you fall in love with the first person you have good sex with?" she asked over the smoky fire. It had drizzled earlier in the day and the wood was wet.

"I don't know. I haven't had good sex. What's it like?" Brook asked with a chortle.

"It's easier with someone who is the same sex, because you know what to do."

"What do you do?" Brook's giggle was contagious.

"You know where all the sensitive places are." Then she broke into laughter.

"Where are they?" Brook was howling now and Sarah joined her.

"Mine are between my legs," she said in a mock whisper, which they both seemed to find very funny. The campground was full. Fires flickered around them.

They rolled on the ground. "Mine too, but it seems only I can find them," Brook said between gasps. "Isn't it amazing what we do when we're caught up in passion? I mean putting our mouths where we'd never think to go otherwise?" This sent them into another laughing frenzy.

Late in the night as Sarah laid in sodden sleep a deep voice whispered in her ear. "I'll put my mouth in those places."

Her eyes popped open. "Hey!" she said, and whoever it was clapped a big hand over her mouth.

Brook was yelling too. "Leave me alone, you pervert."

Someone from outside the tent hollered, "Knock it off or we'll come over there," and the shadows slipped out of the tent.

"Should we go sleep in the car?" Sarah whispered. "I don't feel safe."

"Yeah. Let's lock ourselves in."

It was cramped sleeping, even though Sarah took the backseat and Brook climbed in the front.

The next morning when she hurried to the restroom with a pounding headache, Sarah looked at the surrounding tents, silent in the mist. They would pack up today, but she couldn't help wonder which tent harbored their would-be attackers. She held herself partly responsible.

On the drive back to the condo, they nursed hangovers. The narrowly averted assault had created a gloom not easily shaken. The next morning Sarah would fly back to Wisconsin. Although she wished she could take Brook with her, she was ready to go home.

CHAPTER TWELVE

Summer 2000

Hayley

Coming home from Brown always meant a period of adjustment for Hayley. She was transported from an Ivy League school, where students regularly discussed philosophical questions and played bridge, to her job at Jenkins Gas and Sports Center, where the clientele's main interests were guns and fishing equipment.

The small house she grew up in and the nearby town seemed provincial. She would never invite her schoolmates here, even though she had spent Thanksgiving vacations at their houses, where sometimes there were three forks and spoons and knives next to her plate and a maid serving the food.

Sarah had said she'd arrive on the second Sunday in June, which was Hayley's day off. She was sitting on the raft at the public landing, her arms clasped around her legs. Fast Eddie had dropped her off here. Her brother, Mike, had gone home. She'd asked him to tell their mom that she wouldn't be there for dinner, which meant she might not get supper at all.

The breeze had died, and the lowering sun blazed a trail across the water. When no-wake hours set in, the lake emptied of speeding boats and nature reasserted itself. A flock of geese flew overhead, honking loudly. An eagle sailed above the trees at the east end of the lake.

While watching a little green heron on a neighboring pier, Hayley heard splashing and swiveled to see Sarah swimming toward the raft. Her mouth split into a smile, and the years rolled back. Sarah had been her first best friend, the reason she came home summers instead of finding a job out East and living with a school friend.

Droplets of water clung to her fair skin as Sarah climbed the ladder and sat down next to her. "So how the hell are you?" she asked with a grin, her red eyelashes heavy with water.

"Perfect, now that you're here. What took you so long?" She took Sarah's hand in hers. There was no one around.

"Traffic and a late start. Are you staying the night? It's just me and Mom." Sarah flushed.

Hayley laughed. "I can't wait. Can you? You're the reason I come home."

"Where's Mike? I need a ride to work in the morning."

"You're going to shear trees again? You won't be fit for sex for a week."

"Don't underestimate me."

"How are Brook and Chandler?" She couldn't take her eyes from Sarah's expressive face.

"Chandler is toast, but Brook is great. I invited her for a weekend at the end of June." She was looking into Hayley's eyes. "But she has a job and can't come."

"Too bad," Hayley said, relieved. "When is the rest of the family coming?"

"August. Beth has a serious boyfriend. Jeff has a full-time job. Dad gets restless here." Her mouth drew up in a crooked smile.

They stretched their legs and watched the sun drop toward the trees. A curious contentment settled over Hayley. She never felt this way with anyone else. With others she was always anticipating the next move. When they swam to shore, she took Sarah's hand and led her to the small grove of pines she thought of as their own.

"Maybe we should wait for dark," Sarah said.

"Then Eddie will be here and Mike and maybe some of his friends."

In the enclosure, they kissed as their hands slid quickly into bikini bottoms. When they could no longer stand, they fell to their knees and came quickly. It was then that Hayley tasted guilt. Her roommate at Brown was not toast. She had cried when Hayley went home for the summer.

Hayley had brought a change of clothes. She figured she'd go to Sarah's place and be asked to stay for dinner and spend the night, which was exactly what happened. She was almost as glad to see Sarah's mom as Sarah. She'd had a crush on Kate Sweeney for years. Kate gave her a warm hug when the two girls entered the side door.

"Have dinner with us, Hayley."

"We'll just go upstairs and change, Mom. Do you need any help?"

"Sure."

"Okay. We'll be right down."

They took a couple minutes to grope and kiss while changing before clattering down the stairs. For Hayley it was like the beginning of any other summer since they'd graduated from high school—as if neither of them had ever left. She pushed away the thought that it probably would not be this way again.

Kate said as much when they sat down at the table on the porch overlooking the lake. "You're both seniors now. What are your plans for after graduation, Hayley?"

"I guess I'll look for a newspaper job." When she was at

Brown, it was easy to imagine working in New York or Boston or even Chicago. With Sarah sitting next to her elbow, she was unable to envisage life without summers at the lake.

"Where?" Kate asked.

"I don't know. Where are you going to apply, Sarah?" She already knew the answer.

"The Fox Cities. I've always wanted to live near the lake." Sarah was gazing with great intensity at Hayley. "There is a newspaper there."

She squirmed under the scrutiny. Graduation seemed far away at the moment. "I'll send out inquiries. I write for the university newspaper and the yearbook." She'd always known the day was coming when she and Sarah would go their separate ways. She just hadn't thought much about it.

In bed that night, tucked against each other, Hayley breathed in the smell of the lake in Sarah's hair. She was trying to imagine next summer. Where she would be. What she would be doing.

"You aren't going to look for a job in the Fox Cities, are you? With a degree from Brown you'll probably be working at the *New York Times*."

"That would be a stroke of luck," she scoffed. "If I get a job somewhere besides around here, maybe you can teach at a nearby school."

"Summer will never be the same, will it?" The room was not completely dark. Shadowy trees stood outside the windows. A few stars were visible between the branches.

Hayley hugged Sarah tight. Being with her confused her sometimes. Her desire overwhelmed anything she'd ever felt for anyone else. Her roommate paled in comparison. It was just that when you started having sex, you couldn't always stop—at least she couldn't.

"Let's not talk about next summer, Sarah. Let's enjoy this one."

"It may be our last."

"That'll never happen. I'll find you wherever you go."

"Well, you won't have to look far, because I'll be here on summer weekends. That's my plan."

***

The next morning they both got up early—Sarah to ride to work with Mike and Hayley to go home and get ready for a day at the gas station. This was their routine and as long as Hayley's parents and Kate did not object, she spent her nights at Sarah's.

Nothing much happened at Jenkins's. Nothing much happened at the lake. She went to work. She got home and changed into her swimsuit and walked to the public landing. Sarah met her there.

Eddie and Mike showed up and they water skied till no-wake hours began. Later, they built a fire and sat around it and talked. Somehow, though, the days sped by. Sarah's family arrived, and there was little time for the two young women to be together alone.

They began sneaking off after the fire was doused, but they couldn't stay awake during the day. So they snuck off right after work, but that aroused curiosity. A deep ache developed in Hayley's throat as the time for both Sarah and herself to leave drew close.

The last night they stayed in one of their hideaways as they had for the last three years. Hayley stared at the star-laden sky, listening to Sarah trying not to cry. She rolled on her side and put an arm over her.

"Hey, we'll be so busy, next summer will be here before we know it," she said.

Sarah turned toward her and buried her face in Hayley's neck. "Yeah. And I'll see you at homecoming. Right?"

"I wouldn't miss it."

They were quiet then, pressing against each other, hands and mouths urgently searching. They fell asleep sometime in the night and awakened when the sun cleared the treetops. Pink clouds dotted the sky.

Emerging from the grove of pines, they walked to the shore. The lake lay quiet in the early morning light. They wore swimsuits under their clothes and stripped off the outer layer before wading into the lake. The swim down the beach to Sarah's place was a short one. A great blue heron stood on the raft at the public landing. Yearning filled Hayley's throat and made her mute.

They ate breakfast with Sarah's family and said goodbye on the back porch. Searching Sarah's eyes, Hayley tried to smile. When they hugged, Hayley whispered, "I'll see you, Sweeney."

***

August 2011

When Hayley got to the beach the day Sarah returned from her visit with Brook, she built a fire. She had talked to Sarah earlier, had asked her to pick up a couple of subs, had told her she would be waiting at the public landing. The two weeks Sarah had been gone had seemed like two months.

Her first lover, Constance, had demanded nothing of her. Kristina had been married to Rob, although he too was gay. Her relationship with Sarah was more complicated, filled as it was with memories, and when she stood to greet Sarah, she beat back a surge of emotion.

"Want to share my towel?" she said, not knowing quite how to stop smiling. She was that glad to see Sarah. This was a lonely place without her.

"Later." Sarah gave her a hug, then tore off her T-shirt and shorts and ran whooping into the lake. She disappeared under the raft.

Hayley dropped the beach towel in the sand and followed her. They held onto the anchor rope and kissed. The sun set, leaving a smear of red along the horizon, before they swam to shore. The fire had burned to pulsing hot coals, and Hayley fed it from the kindling stacked next to the steps. When the wood crackled and burst into flames, they ducked into a grove of pines and took off their suits, pulling on dry shorts and T-shirts.

"Thanks for the food," Hayley said as they ate. She thought nothing had tasted so good. She was so hungry.

"No problem." Sarah leaned into the fire, her face and hair glowing red in the glare.

"Guess who's coming Sunday," Hayley said, bracing herself.

"Who?"

"Eddie. He's bringing the boat." She watched Sarah stiffen.

"How did that happen?"

"He called and left a message with Mom."

Sarah's eyes betrayed her anger. "I don't want to see him."

She met Sarah's heated gaze. "It's our chance for revenge."

"How?"

"I'll tell you later. Let's not talk about him right now," she said.

Sarah stared into the fire. "Anyone else coming down tonight?"

"You mean like Mike? No." She lay back on the old blanket she'd brought, arms under her head. A half moon floated among a sea of stars. Insects buzzed from the grasses and trees. Her love for this place, which she hadn't even realized until she left and thought she'd shed it, surfaced. Where else had she seen such a sky?

She pulled Sarah down beside her and placed an arm over her. "I have to work tomorrow."

They fell asleep, and when they wakened, the moon was low in the western sky. The fire had again burned to coals. Hayley wrapped them in the blanket, and they made love in its confines. Neither wore anything under her T-shirts and shorts. It was easy to slide a hand up the inside of Sarah's thigh. Like herself, she was so ready.

Sunlight was shafting through the trees and across the lake when they awoke again. Its warmth hadn't yet reached them. The fire was cold. She poured lake water on it anyway. They kept an empty milk jug by the woodpile for that purpose. It was almost six according to the watch in Hayley's pocket.

"Got to go." She gave Sarah a quick kiss, threw her damp suit in her beach towel, stepped into flip-flops and galloped up the steps. At the top she turned. "See you around four either here or at your place. Bring the blanket."

She walked into the modest ranch house where she had grown up and tiptoed past her parents' closed door to her childhood bedroom. She was sure they were just as dismayed by her return home as she was. After all, she'd had a Cadillac education.

Her walls bore the posters of her youth—k.d.lang, Melissa Etheridge and Bonnie Raitt, still favorites of hers. She'd put up pictures of Dave Matthews and Michael Jackson to throw off any suspicion that she might prefer women to men. How stupid was that?

In and out of the shower in minutes, she was drying her hair when her mom knocked on the bathroom door and said, "Morning."

"Did I wake you?" she asked in the kitchen where she grabbed a banana. She'd get coffee at the gas station.

"Nope. Will you be here for dinner tonight?"

"I don't know. Don't wait for me."

"She could come for dinner too. Anytime." By "she" her mom meant Sarah.

"Maybe next time." She gave her mother a peck on the cheek, which brought a smile to her face. She was going out the door when her dad appeared.

"Have a good one," he said.

"I'll try." She drove her dad's old truck, the one he used for hauling wood and other dirty jobs. She was at work behind the counter at five to seven.

The day inched by in degrees of seconds or so it seemed, although there was a constant stream of customers—filling up their vehicles, buying bait and tackle and hunting gear, lining up for oil changes and tire rotations and even getting fishing licenses this late in the season. She was busy enough, but it made a difference that Sarah was only a few miles away. She longed to be with her, sunning or reading or swimming.

She understood Sarah's confusion and anger when she'd moved back home. She was ashamed of the way she'd behaved after leaving New York. Perhaps it had been a mistake not to move in with Sarah, but she had needed to find a job quick and the only way she saw to do that was to ask Jenkins to take her back—at least for the rest of the vacation season. There was always the possibility of returning to New York City.

The column she wrote for the local weekly newspaper paid a pittance, but it was getting her name out there. Her last article had been a hit. She'd been driving toward the lake from town when she'd come upon a huge turkey cock strutting around in the middle of the blacktop. She could hardly believe her eyes. This was a relatively busy road. So she turned on her flashers and got out of the truck to chase the turkey to safety. "Go on. Get off the road," she shouted, waving her arms.

With a bare blinking eye and swinging wattles, it turned on her. She let out a shriek and fled from the beak on the outstretched neck. The bird had been almost as tall as she was and rocketed toward her with frightening speed. The encounter would have been comical had she not been so scared. At the time, she'd been anything but amused. Her readers were, though. Later she learned this turkey had a harem of females and was too familiar with people to be afraid of them.

However, a column in the weekly newspaper was not enough to convince potential employers that she was employable. She had gone to the public library in Waushara and asked if she could have the use of one of their meeting rooms to hold a night class on how to blog. The librarian gave her the go-ahead but told her she couldn't charge a fee. So she turned to the high school and made the same request of her old principal and was given the same answer. Only then did she approach Shirley Newcomb, the owner of the New and Used Bookstore, and ask if she could use the back room.

"What's in it for me?" Shirley had gone to high school with her, had once been a cheerleader and was now a large woman who would never do the splits again.

"A percentage of the fee."

"How much?"

"Whatever you think is fair." She considered the how-to-blog class a pretty original idea, especially in these parts.

"Charge thirty bucks a person. I'll take twenty percent. If no one comes, I still get a lesson."

Impressed by Shirley's decisiveness, she'd said, "Okay. I'll get the word out. Maybe you can put a sign-up sheet here in the store." She would write the next column for free in exchange for the advertising.

Already ten women and two men had signed up, including one of her old high school teachers. She talked to Shirley about doing a creative writing class after the blogging one, but Shirley thought they should cut off the enrollment and run another how-to-blog class on the heels of the first one, which would start the Tuesday night after Labor Day weekend.

When she got to the public beach after work, Eddie's new Ski Nautique was anchored offshore. Sarah was nowhere in sight. She shaded her eyes and glared at Eddie, who seemed to be asleep behind the wheel. He splashed into the lake as she hurried toward Sarah's.

He trotted up to her, droplets of water clinging to his body hair. "Hey, wait up."

She walked faster, but his legs were longer. "What are you doing here? I thought you were coming tomorrow."

"I came early. We still have an hour to ski."

She whirled on him. "You can't come with me to Sarah's place."

"Why?" he asked, looking truly perplexed.

"Because she doesn't want you there."

"Why?"

"Make a stab in the dark, Eddie. If you wait here, maybe I can get her to come."

"Okay. I'll build a fire. I've got a little picnic for us. Toasted wienies, potato salad and slaw from the deli."

When no one was on Sarah's beach, she knocked on the screen door. "Anyone home?"

Pat opened the door. "I thought you were family. Family doesn't knock."

Hayley pushed the dog's nose out of her crotch. She figured he was getting her scent and made a little joke. "Guess he thinks I'm a stray."

"Sit." Pat pulled on Junior's collar. "I read your column about that old turkey. I don't suppose you thought it was so funny at the time, but it made me laugh. Kate tried to shoo him off the road once too."

"I saw that you're teaching a class," Kate called from the kitchen. "Good for you."

"Yeah. Twelve people have signed up." She wouldn't get rich, but every little bit helped.

"What class?" Sarah asked, coming down the stairs.

"How to blog." She would have told Sarah, but she wasn't sure whether anyone would sign up. She didn't want to look like a loser.

A frown crossed Sarah's face. "But you never said…"

"I know. It's a night class at the New and Used Bookstore. Hey, it's nice out. Why don't you put on your suit and go for a swim with me?"

"I just took it off."

"Come on, Sarah. I've been stuck inside all week."

"Okay, but we'll have to swim here."

Hayley waited downstairs with Pat and Kate, answering questions about the class. She knew they had no plans to start a blog, that they were only interested in her.

Once they were out the door, Sarah said she'd seen Eddie at the public beach and she wasn't going down there.

"Eddie has a picnic waiting for us. This is what we're going to do." And she told Sarah.

"What if he doesn't fall for it?"

"He will. Trust me. First, though, we'll get free food and drink."

***

A fire flickered inside the pile of stones. "Hey," Eddie said in greeting. "Want to ski first? We have half an hour." He grinned, looking deceptively boyish.

She glanced at Sarah, who shook her head.

"Tomorrow."

Eddie began taking containers out of the cooler and setting them on the lid—potato salad, coleslaw and a package of wieners and buns along with ketchup and Dijon mustard. "Let's eat then." He put four wienies on a long fork and pointed at a bag. "Want to get out the paper plates and napkins? The beer is in the other cooler."

She and Sarah sat cross-legged on the blanket and ate the food. They washed it down with beer. When they were done, Eddie packed the leftovers in the cooler, burned the paper stuff and sacked the rest. The sun was low in the west but far from gone.

Hayley suggested a ride in his boat. No wake, of course. She banked the fire. Sarah hung back with her, while Eddie carried the cooler out to the boat.

"I feel kind of bad. He went to all that trouble."

"You mean you've forgiven him?"

"No."

Eddie waited in the Ski Nautique. The women clambered into the boat. "Just like the old folks. They always idle around the lake at sunset."

As if on cue, a crowded pontoon boat rounded the end of the lake, heading toward them.

Eddie rolled a joint and passed it around, along with more beer. Sarah was already glassy-eyed. Hayley's ears buzzed. If they got too high, they'd never be able to carry out her plan.

The boat slowly cruised the shoreline. Hayley sat in the back with Sarah. Both refused any more beer and the last few draws from Eddie's joint. The smell of marijuana overpowered all the good smells.

Hayley was always surprised at how quickly the sun disappeared. One minute half of it hovered over the trees, like a huge egg yolk, the next it sank out of sight. Eddie anchored and they waded to shore. He put a few sticks on the fire and it blazed. The night was warm.

"Good night to skinny dip," Hayley said.

Eddie snapped to attention. "Want to?" he asked eagerly.

"Why not?" She looked at Sarah, who was swaying and said nothing.

"Ready?" Hayley pulled her T-shirt off and dropped her shorts.

Apparently that was enough motivation for Eddie. He jerked his T-shirt over his head and stepped out of his trunks. For a moment he stood facing them, his naked skin glowing in the firelight. Then he ran waist deep into the water and dove.

"Come on," she hissed at Sarah, who was standing as if stuck to the ground. Hayley scooped up Eddie's clothes and ran down the beach, where she threw them into a bunch of bushes along the shore.

When they got to Sarah's door, huffing with the effort and excitement, Hayley looked down the steps toward the lake. She saw no one and hurried inside behind Sarah. Pat and Kate looked up from where they were sitting on the porch. Hayley knew she was impaired and if she was, Sarah must be on the verge of unconsciousness.

"What's happening?" Pat asked.

Hayley hadn't thought this far ahead and backed toward the stairs, hoping to make it without notice to Sarah's bedroom where they could change out of their reeking clothes. She froze at the knock on the door.

"You want to get that?" Kate said.

The dog barked. Sarah leaned against the stair wall.

"I'll get it." Pat turned on the outside light and took a few steps backward. The screen door hid nothing.

Hayley had a perfect view of Eddie standing naked on the doorstep. Sarah thumped down on one of the bottom steps and whooped with laughter.

"It's not funny. Where are my clothes?" Eddie said indignantly.

Kate got up to see what was going on. She hushed the dog, grabbing his collar. "What...?"

"You want to tell him where his clothes are?" Pat asked, turning toward the younger women.

Hayley looked at Sarah and lost all control. Neither could utter a word. They doubled over, clutching their middles.

Eddie pulled on the door handle, but the screen was locked. "Why'd you do it?" He seemed truly perplexed.

Their laughs turned into occasional snorts. Finally Hayley managed to say, "They're in the bushes."

He turned and disappeared into the night. The sight of his bare bottom sent the two of them into more gales of laughter.

Pat shut the door and returned to the porch without a word, but Kate looked at her daughter and Hayley for a long moment before saying, "Aren't you two a little old for this?"

It only made them laugh harder, and she too went back to the porch.

The thought of displeasing Sarah's mom quickly sobered Hayley. She grabbed Sarah's arm. "Come on. Let's get out of these smelly clothes."

They staggered up the steps to Sarah's bedroom where they

fell on the bed and laughed until Sarah suddenly rushed to the john. Hayley heard her barfing. She came back carrying the wastebasket and was moaning when Hayley fell asleep.

***

She woke up when the sun blazed a trail across the bed. Her mouth tasted of stale beer and smoke. When she stood up, the room spun. "Whoa," she said, plopping back down. Slowly, she got to her feet again and made her way to the bathroom. She peed, ate some toothpaste and drank out of the faucet before returning and climbing back in bed.

Sarah turned toward her, mouth open, emitting puffs of dragon breath. She let out a little snort, and Hayley pulled the sheet over their bodies before turning her back. The house was quiet, and she fell asleep again, but not before noticing the room smelled of vomit and marijuana.

Kate and Pat were drinking coffee on the porch when she and Sarah went downstairs. Kate called from the porch. "Help yourself to coffee. You must need it."

"We're taking it down to the beach," Sarah said.

"Better eat something, even if it's toast," Kate advised.

Sarah looked at her. "Want a piece of toast? I'm not sure I can keep one down."

"You better try," Hayley said.

"What if he's down there?"

Hayley shrugged. "We'll tell him why."

"You want to tell us?" Kate asked, and Hayley wondered that she heard them.

"He spied on us," she said.

"Spied on you?" Sarah's mom asked.

Pat said something neither Sarah nor Hayley heard and Kate said, "Oh."

They took their toast and coffee out into the morning. The sun was already hot at nine o'clock. Settling gingerly into a chair, Hayley looked down the beach and saw Eddie's boat anchored at the public beach. "He hasn't left."

While they ate and sipped the hot black liquid, Eddie started the Ski Nautique and made his way to Sarah's pier. Hayley felt a kind of admiration for his audacity. Would she have the nerve to stand outside anyone's door naked? And then turn up the next day? Even the questions were laughable.

He'd found his swim trunks and shirt, she saw, as he stood up to grab a pier post. "Want to ski?"

She glanced at Sarah, who looked nonplussed. "He's too forgiving. I don't trust him."

Eddie fastened the boat and walked toward them. "Got any more coffee?"

Without a word Sarah climbed the steps. Hayley wondered if she would come back. She shielded her eyes from the sun.

Eddie sat where Sarah had been. "Why?" he asked.

"You spied on us and you asked others if they wanted to watch."

"Who told you that?"

"Jeff told Sarah."

"Are we even now?"

"It's up to Sarah. If she comes back down with coffee, I suppose we are."

Sarah brought a thermos of coffee. After they drank it, Hayley skied and Mike came down to the public beach to join them. It took Hayley back to the last summer they were all together.

CHAPTER THIRTEEN

2011

The electricity went off the Friday morning of Labor Day weekend, during seventy-plus straight-line winds. Hayley looked worriedly out the windows at the bending trees across the street. When the gas pumps and computers shut down, Jenkins started up the generator so that a few lights burned and the air pump in the minnow tank circulated oxygen.

When his wife called to say a tree had fallen on their garage, he told Hayley to go home, he was locking up. Paper and signs and dirt were flying across the pavement like bullets. Hayley covered her face with her arm to protect her eyes as she scurried to her truck. Her phone was ringing, and she put it to her ear as she sat behind the wheel. The door slammed and the truck rocked in the wind as rain beat on its roof, making it hard to hear.

"How are you?"

"Kristina?" she said with disbelief. "I can't talk. I'm in the middle of a storm." She realized it had been a mistake to leave the gas station.

"Rob moved out."

"Yeah. Well, I can't deal with that right now. I have to get home."

"I need to talk to you."

"About what? You kicked me out. Remember?"

"Will you come back if I send you money?"

"No."

"Wait. Where are you?" If Kristina hadn't sounded so uncharacteristically unnerved, she wouldn't have told her.

"Back home. Got to go." And she shut the phone.

It rang most of the way to the house as the rain and wind battered the old truck. She gripped the steering wheel, fighting to keep the vehicle on the pavement. She turned onto the access road, thinking she was home safe, and hit the brakes hard. A tree was lying in the middle of the blacktop. When she put the truck in reverse, another tree crashed down behind her. Rigid with tension, she slowly reversed around that one and took the back circle to the house.

There was no room in the garage for the old truck, so she parked outside as the double door rose. Her dad stood inside, his hands on his hips, and she ran for safety—drenched in those few seconds.

"We were worried," he said.

"I couldn't answer the phone and drive."

Her mom stood in the kitchen. "You're home." Relief was in her voice.

Hayley stripped off her wet clothes in the bathroom and changed into dry ones before checking her voice mail—Sarah, her parents and Kristina.

She called Sarah. "Don't you have orientation today?"

"They sent us home. No electricity. More than forty thousand people are without power here. How about you?"

She told her about closing the gas station, probably the first time in its history, and the harrowing drive home. A tree in the backyard split with a loud crack, making her jump. Half of it fell, bouncing as it hit the ground. "Have you called your mom?"

"Yeah. They're sitting tight. So far no trees have fallen on the buildings."

"One just missed the house here."

The phone rang as soon as she snapped it shut.

"Are you home now?" Kristina asked.

"Barely. Why did Rob leave?"

"He moved in with his boyfriend. He wants a divorce." Her voice broke.

She'd never understood their marriage and wasn't sympathetic. "He's gay. He can marry his boyfriend now."

"You could marry me."

"I can't marry you, Kristina. I don't love you that way."

"You could have fooled me. Look, I have to see you."

"I'm living at home. You can't come here." She panicked at the thought of Kristina appearing on her doorstep.

"Why not?"

"Because this isn't New York City and my parents don't know you're anyone but a friend."

"Well, I'll be your friend from New York."

"I've got a job. I don't have time."

"Do they have a motel in Waushara? Isn't that the name of the nearest town?"

"There's no electricity. The power could be out for days." How did Kristina remember that when she never seemed to recall anything else about Hayley? There was a motel across from the gas station, but she couldn't think of its name. She'd always wondered how it stayed in business when the biggest event in town was the snowmobile watercross over the millpond in the middle of summer. Of course, the snowmobiles seldom made it across and had to be pulled out of the water. It was dumber than dumb.

"I've got a few days off next week."

"And I've got a girlfriend here."

"Sarah, right? Didn't you tell me she was a childhood friend?"

"She's my lover. You never get over your first love. Forget me. Okay?" She was whispering and hung up after saying, "Goodbye, Kristina."

When the winds died down and the rain stopped, her dad started up the chainsaw and cleared a tree that had scraped the old truck on its way down. She moved the cut wood out of the way and then went with him to help remove the downed trees blocking the road.

Afterward, they checked the driveways on the back road and the ones that led to the summer homes on the lake. A dead oak had fallen halfway down Kate's driveway. Pat and Kate were trying to roll it to the side. With a nod, Hayley's dad fired up the chainsaw.

"Hey, thanks," Kate said when the wood was off the drive.

"You fixed for water?" Hayley's dad asked.

"We're hauling it up from the lake. How about you?" Pat said.

"That's what we'll have to do. It's a good thing we've got muscles here." He put his arm around Hayley.

She flashed back to graduation at Brown. She'd been embarrassed by her parents, who were obviously not rich—their clothes and haircuts and accents indicative of where they lived. Now she was ashamed of herself.

"Ready?" her dad asked.

"Yep."

"Thanks again, Ralph."

"You bet," he said.

Her dad drove along the north side of the lake, cutting more downed trees that blocked driveways. Before they went home, they filled containers with water from the lake and hauled them up the short hill to the truck. When they turned into their own driveway, Hayley was tired and dirty and feeling good. She stepped down from the truck and went inside where her mom had food waiting. She ate like she was starved.

"I'm going back out," her dad said when he got up from the table. "There are plenty of places we didn't get to."

"I'll come," she volunteered. The food had given her energy.

"I'll come too," her mom said. "There's nothing to do here."

They made it halfway around the lake before darkness settled in. Her dad had to siphon gas out of the truck and mix it with oil for the saw. Some tried to pay him, and Hayley thought he should accept it. At first, he refused, but when the owners were obviously wealthy, he took a five when it was offered.

Mike's Jeep was parked in the driveway when they got home. "You should have waited for me."

"There's still plenty to do," their dad said.

When their mom and dad left the room, Mike said, "I suppose Dad was playing superhero, clearing all the driveways around the lake."

"Yeah, so? He was helping people."

"He's no spring chicken nor is Mom."

Their dad worked as a machinist and welder in the county highway department. His arms were ropy with muscles. Their mom was a data processor at the courthouse. She had never thought of either as being at risk.

"He seemed fine. So did Mom. Exercise is good for them."

"But Dad never knows when to quit. He does believe he's Superman."

She didn't want to think of her dad as vulnerable, but what did she know? She hadn't been here. She'd never have time to make up for all the years she'd been gone. "Did something happen?"

"No, but next time make him wait for me."

"I'm not going to live here forever. Besides, I'm almost as good help as you are."

He smiled. "Yeah, almost."

***

Saturday morning when Mike went out with their dad to clear more driveways, she stayed home to blog. She worked at the old desk where she'd done her schoolwork when she was a kid.

Voucher schools were meant for lower income kids who were failing in the Milwaukee public schools, she wrote. *Despite their poor performance, these schools have been expanded to Racine. They have also been opened up to children of every income level.*

She pointed out that while public schools would have to

make do with $800 million less from the state, public taxes would pay over $6,000 in tuition per student for these private schools, many of which were religious ones. Critics saw voucher schools as part of a nationwide effort to break public schools and the teachers' unions. Hayley saw them as a nationwide effort to privatize schools. She put the information on her blog.

She shut off her computer to save battery power and called Sarah, whose power had come back on Friday night. She'd chosen to stay at the apartment, rather than be one more person who would have to use lake water to wash dishes and flush the toilet.

"Are you coming home next weekend?"

"If Mom has electricity, I will."

"We better have it by then."

"Depends on the weather too. If it's cold and you're working on Saturday, I might stay here."

Hayley wasn't sure how many weekends she could get through without Sarah. With no real friends and nothing to do besides work at the gas station and on her blog the days ahead of her looked bleak. "Come on, Sarah. That'll be two weekends in a row, and you just got back from Washington."

"You could come here, you know."

"Maybe I will."

***

When Hayley left Shirley's New and Used Bookstore, she felt good. Everyone in the class had set up a weblog and created their "about me" page. Some had even written their first post. Personal stuff mostly—family, favorite hobby. There was one guy, Herman Jablonski, who wrote about how concealed carry made everyone safer. She didn't want to be the person who helped him get his message out. Who do you conceal your gun from, if not a person? She left through the back door with Shirley and waited for her to lock up. "It went well, didn't you think?" she asked.

"A huge success." One streetlamp lit the alley. "I don't like going out here alone at night."

"What could happen? We're in Waushara, not New York City," she said.

"It probably comes from reading too many mysteries. See you next Tuesday." Shirley settled her bulk in her Chrysler van.

Hayley drove the back roads home. The night was dark, the pavement black. She watched the shoulders for the glint of eyes. She didn't want to hit any animal, especially not a deer. She no longer sped heedlessly through the night as she had in her youth.

The first time Sarah yelled for her to stop so that she could pick up a turtle crossing the road and carry it safely to the other side, she'd laughed. But turtles die hard. Sarah had once said she'd rather see some people as roadkill in place of the animals they ran over so carelessly and left to rot.

***

Kristina called her at work the next day. The power had been restored countywide late Monday. Hayley was wiping down the counters when her phone vibrated in her pocket. She put the cell to her ear, wondering whether she was going to get blasted or wooed. She never knew with Kristina.

"Rob moved in with his boyfriend," were her first words.

"You told me he was going to, and besides, it's about time," she replied. There was no need to tiptoe around Kristina anymore.

"Where are you?"

"At work. I can't talk long."

"Where is work?"

Hayley hesitated to tell her. She knew she'd be appalled, and she was.

"You're a journalist, Hayley, not a gas station attendant."

"I'm both right now. The gas station pays more."

"Come back to New York where you belong. This town you live in is barely on the map."

"We don't live in town."

"Constance is horrified by your move."

"You initiated it. Did you tell her you kicked me out?" A truck pulled up to one of the pumps. "I have to go, Kristina. The customers always come first."

The number of customers always tapered off after Labor

Day weekend. Any day she was expecting Jenkins to tell her he didn't need her or he only wanted her to work part-time.

The week dragged by, getting warmer as it drew to an end. She focused on work and her blog, since she could only talk to Sarah at night now and often Sarah was busy with schoolwork. Reading all the comments on the blog and posting her own took a large part of the evening. She sometimes nodded off over her laptop.

While she was leaning on the counter at work late Saturday morning, two women got out of a small car. Only when they came through the door did she really believe they were Constance and Kristina—both dressed in tight-fitting straight leg jeans, leather jackets and high heel boots. She stared at them, speechless with surprise, as they paused to eye the hunting garb and equipment with amazed expressions. She was both mortified and amused as she waited for them to see her. Outside, a truck pulled up to one of the pumps. Jenkins was showing a customer the archery equipment.

Kristina looked startled when their eyes met. She tapped Constance, who zeroed in on Hayley. As they approached, Constance said, "We stopped at the first gas station and here you are." She wore her gray-streaked black hair long and squiggly. There was a lot of it, and it made a wonderful frame for her high cheekbones and piercing brown eyes.

"You found me. The question is why."

"Like I said, you're a journalist, not a gas station attendant." Kristina's hazel eyes homed in on Hayley. Her hair fell in a black wave to her chin.

"Like I said, I'm both. This job pays better."

"We're going to check into the motel across the street. Why don't you come over after work and we'll go to dinner together?" Constance suggested.

The person who had filled his tank paid at the pump and drove off. Hayley's boss left the archer and made his way to where she stood with the two women. "Friends of yours, Hayley?"

"Yes. This is my boss, Walt Jenkins." She smiled sweetly as she introduced the women, gesturing as she did so. "Constance Lindstrom and Kristina Berken came all this way from New York City."

Mr. Jenkins's gaze settled on Constance. How could he resist her? She screamed elegance. Kristina would never personify the word, but Hayley had to admit she made a fashion statement. To them, Hayley was sure, she had reverted to the role of a redneck, dressed as she was in regular jeans and a sweatshirt that advertised the store—a twelve-point buck with the words *Jenkins Sports Center* under it.

Jenkins chatted with them until the archer signaled for his attention. "Excuse me, ladies. Business calls."

The two women left to check into the motel, after exacting a promise from Hayley that she would come over when she got off work. The last hour of her shift flew by in a flurry of customers. Where they came from she had no idea. This was usually a dead time of day. On her way across the street, she called her mom to tell her she'd be home late, not to hold dinner.

Kristina let her into the room. She was holding a plastic hotel tumbler in one hand. "Let me pour you some wine. It's from a gas station further down the road—a Robert Mondavi cabernet. Not too bad, believe it or not. A little fruity." She considered herself a wine connoisseur.

Constance was propped up on two pillows on one of the beds, her loosely curled hair spread across the white pillowcase. Hayley remembered the first time they had bedded, how it had opened her eyes to the world of lesbian sex. She relived the thrill and felt naked again as Constance observed her over her reading glasses.

Sitting on one of the two chairs, she accepted the Robert Mondavi from Kristina. "Thanks. I haven't had a glass of wine since I left New York. I usually drink beer." Was that true? Kate and Pat often served wine before and at dinner.

The other two women's noses wrinkled in distaste, and Hayley laughed. "Wisconsin is a big beer and brandy state."

"From now on when I see one of those monstrous-looking cheeses on someone's head, I will think of you," Kristina said.

"You are such a snob. You come from New Jersey," she said lightly, feeling a need to defend the home she had once told Sarah was too provincial.

"At least New Jersey is within commuting distance of New York City."

Constance took off her glasses and gazed at Hayley. "You have a talent that might well be wasted here."

"In this backwater?" Hayley finished for her.

"I didn't say that. It's just that your message might not get out."

"I'm on the web. I actually have a following. Ed Schultz started out as a sportscaster in North Dakota. Look where he is now." She had seen the documentary, *Broadcast Blues*, by Sue Wilson—about how the FCC wasn't accountable to the public when it came to talk radio. She'd also googled Schultz and found out he'd been a Republican in his earlier years before he started working for MSNBC.

"But you're going backward," Kristina pointed out.

"Are you here to save me?" She looked from one to the other.

"You can live with me or Kristina." Constance smiled benignly.

"Aren't you with someone?" She couldn't bear to witness Constance's love affairs.

"Does it matter?" Constance thought talking about such things was vulgar.

"To me it does."

"Well, *I'm* not with anyone," Kristina said.

"Not yet. I would always wonder when you might decide to throw me out again." She looked out the window at the gas station and the pond across the road to ground herself. "I could give you a tour of my home turf."

"Why don't you do that tomorrow?" Constance said.

"There's a really good restaurant in town." Which was quite amazing. It had once been a bar with a four-lane bowling alley.

"We'll let you decide," Constance said. "You know the area best."

Kristina opened a box of water crackers and a container of Brie, which she must have brought with her. Hayley would have devoured it all, along with the wine, but she held herself back, not wanting to look uncouth. After downing two tumblers of wine in the plastic glasses the motel provided, she felt slightly lightheaded. It made her think of Sarah after she consumed a couple of beers and a joint. She smiled.

As if on cue, Kristina said, "Does your girlfriend, Sarah, live around here?"

"She's an hour away in Appleton." She smiled wryly, again thinking of the long winter.

"What do you do here for entertainment?" Constance asked.

"Swim and water ski in the summer, ski or snowshoe in the winter. There are a ton of people who fish and hunt. There are plays and symphonies and stuff like that at the Performing Arts Center in Appleton. Lawrence College gives free concerts."

"Why don't you live in Appleton?" Kristina asked.

"This is where my job is." She felt a bit defensive now and could hear it in her tone.

Constance held up a hand, "You've moved back home for more than a few weeks then."

"I have." Still defensive. "I won't be here forever, but I'm not going to live off Sarah or anyone else."

"Is there nothing we can say to convince you to come back to New York?"

"Not now." Had they really thought their presence would make her pack up and move without a job or prospect of one? She was flattered that they had bothered.

"So, let's make the best of it," Constance said. She sat up and her tangle of hair settled around her shoulders. Hayley could almost feel it—the gray strands coarser than the black.

She was still reeling from their sudden appearance, from knowing that they thought she'd made a huge mistake. She wished Sarah was here for backup but also so that she could show off her ex-lovers. When her phone rang, startling her—she'd thought it was on vibrate—and she saw Sarah's name in the display, it was as if she'd conjured her up.

"Can I call you later?"

"I'm at Mom's."

She sat up straight. "You are?" she said, wondering how she was going to do this and plunged on before any doubts assailed her. "Can you come to the inn across from Jenkins's, not the hotel on the pond?"

"Good idea. We can get a room."

"Sarah? There are a couple of people here I want you to meet."

"Who?"

"Let me surprise you."

"I don't like surprises that should come with a warning."

"Constance and Kristina."

"Oh." Hayley heard the worry in that one little word.

"It's okay, Sarah. I want them to meet you." She had turned her back and lowered her voice for privacy.

"Any way I can get out of this?"

"No."

***

Sarah's reddish hair shone, her cheeks were flushed, her skin unblemished, her eyes bright—more blue than gray. She wore nice slacks and a top that showed just enough cleavage. Hayley pulled her into the room and kissed her lightly on the mouth. "It is *so* good to see you," she whispered.

"Well, thanks." Sarah looked past her at the other two women.

She never would have guessed, had she not known her well, that Sarah was nervous—a slightly forced smile, a stiffness in her posture.

She imagined Constance through Sarah's wide eyes. Constance had tamed her hair as much as possible. Her clothes, her walk, her gestures showed off a self-contained sensuality—at least to Hayley. Kristina was a little brittle but beautiful all the same.

In turn the two women took Sarah's proffered hand and kissed her cheek. Kristina poured her a glass of wine. "Sit down. We're playing Scrabble. Constance always carries a travel version with her."

Sarah had played for years with her mother and sister. Hayley knew she carried a dictionary of Scrabble words in her head. They had called the motel management for two more chairs, and now they started over.

When Sarah easily beat them all, Constance looked at her with a wry smile of admiration. "You are good at this."

Sarah shrugged modestly. "I've had lots of practice. My mom plays it often."

"Kate," Constance said, and Sarah looked startled, then glanced at Hayley.

The Vintage Café was just down the street. They walked there as the sun set; the red sky over the millpond was reflected in the still water, the streets empty except for cars lined up outside the bars. Inside the Vintage they explored the antiques up front and along the walls in the long dining room that had once been the bowling alley. The menu posted at the entryway to the dining room was limited, but Hayley knew the food was good as was the wine selection.

Constance said after eating a few bites, "Excellent. How do they survive in this tiny village?"

"If this place were in New York, it would be mobbed," Kristina added.

"We appreciate good food too," Hayley said, savoring their surprise at finding it here where they least expected it.

Sarah had no comment. The Fox Cities had lots of good restaurants. She winked at Hayley, and Hayley swallowed a laugh.

The owner came to their table when they ordered dessert and coffee. Both Sarah and Hayley knew her by name, and Hayley introduced her to Constance and Kristina, who were gracious.

"Wonderful food," Constance said. "A real treat."

Kristina agreed. "A place like this would thrive in New York City."

The owner smiled. "I'm glad you're trying the desserts. We make everything here. Enjoy your stay." She looked at Hayley and Sarah and smiled. "Have you shown them around?"

"Tomorrow," Hayley said.

Stuffed, they walked back to the motel under the streetlights.

She and Sarah had checked into the Inn. They sat on one of the beds with hips and shoulders touching. She asked, "Where should we take them tomorrow?"

"We?" Sarah asked and smiled mischievously. "Why don't you introduce them to your parents and my mom and Pat and show them the lake, then maybe take them on a tour of the lakes. Don't forget the Mount Morris Ski Hill and the fish hatchery. I think the hatchery is the biggest in the state. What time do they leave?"

She laughed aloud about touring the fish hatchery. She pictured Kristina and Constance wobbling along beside the holding ponds, gazing at schools of fish, their eyes glazed over with boredom. "I didn't ask. How long can you stay?"

"Five or so."

She flopped onto her back. "I am so full."

Lying down next to her, Sarah asked, "Why are they here?" She turned to look at Hayley.

"They're trying to get me to move back to New York."

"They believe your talents are wasted here. Is that it?" she asked with thinly veiled irony.

"Kristina thinks so much of me that she threw me out of the apartment. Rob left her and moved in with his boyfriend, like he should have done a long time ago. Now she wants me back, no doubt to help pay the rent."

"They're both stunning," Sarah said, her gaze fixed on Hayley's. She was one of those people who thought she could see the truth in someone's eyes.

"You're tastier," Hayley said and then wished she could take it back.

"You would know, wouldn't you?"

She kept her eyes on Sarah's. "Does it matter? That was then, this is now." But something in her still yearned for Constance. She hadn't gotten her fill.

They rolled toward each other, and Hayley focused on Sarah's mouth, warm and giving. Even as they kissed, she was fantasizing about her first time with Constance. How shocked and enthralled she'd been. She had barely been able to respond, had stood stiffly while Constance undressed her and herself, not knowing where to look or what to do—even after all those summers of sex with Sarah.

To get it on with Constance at first she'd had to get mentally past their bodies into a realm that was created by the physical yet went beyond it—a state of such intense ecstasy that she was aware of nothing else. Constance had known how to make her ache with pleasure.

Now she made love to Sarah as Constance had first made love to her. Sarah wasn't a limp recipient—she threw herself into the act enthusiastically—but neither was she Constance with years of experience. It occurred to Hayley that she probably came up short in comparison too, and she wondered if the other two women were doing the same thing in the next room.

When they lay catching their breath in the messy tangle of nubby sheets, Hayley realized she didn't care what Constance and Kristina were doing. She turned her head toward Sarah and stretched languorously. "What made you decide to come to the lake?"

"Besides missing you?" Sarah said with an answering grin before turning serious. "The school board panel that decides whether to include challenged reading material is reviewing *The Catcher in the Rye*. I had to put it on hold. It's a classic, Hayley. I read that book when I was fifteen or sixteen. I loved it."

"I read it too, about the same time you did. Why would anyone object to it?"

"Who knows? They'd ban any book that had sex in it or cussing or an original thought. They claim Holden is antisocial."

"I wonder what Holden would have said about iPhones and Facebook."

"That most of the stuff on it is callow and phony. Was he iconoclastic? Or was he just an idealist?"

"He was a teenager, and this isn't class." She kissed Sarah, ready to start over, but when she realized Sarah wanted to talk, she asked, "What else is on your reading list?" Sarah taught an American literature class.

"Michael Dorris's *Yellow Raft on Blue Water*, *To Kill a Mockingbird*, *A Farewell to Arms*, *The Good Earth* and *The Grapes of Wrath*."

"I don't think I ever read Michael Dorris."

"He was married to author Louise Erdrich until their daughters accused him of abuse, both physical and sexual, and he killed himself."

"Wow. Was he guilty?"

"I don't think there was a trial, but Erdrich admitted to the physical abuse. Both wrote about Native Americans. She is one. His claims are unsubstantiated. He adopted Native American kids, though. They all had fetal alcohol syndrome."

"You are full of all kinds of information."

"It's all on the web, but I really liked the book. I doubt the panel will object to my other books. They're too established as classics."

"These people who want to decide what our kids can read, who we can sleep with, whether schools should teach sex education or abstinence, whether we can use birth control or have an abortion have been running for school boards, city councils and state legislatures for years. Now they're in positions to make those decisions." It would be her next blog. "Oh, and they're the ones who don't want to regulate corporations or Wall Street."

"I just had to get away. There are all these new faces at school. Most of those who retired did so because we lost collective bargaining rights. A lot of them were really good teachers."

She gave up trying to arouse Sarah and rolled on her back again, which was when Sarah began to caress her—idly at first and then with more interest. Around midnight they fell asleep.

***

In the morning they drove separate cars. Constance rode with Hayley. She looked out the window with interest. "Pretty country," she said after five minutes. "All the pines and that little lake we just passed that was so blue-green."

"That's because it's deep, and it's deep because it's a no-wake lake. None of our lakes are really big around here, and the speedboats cause the shores to erode into the water. In a one thousand-acre lake it doesn't matter. In a one hundred fifty-acre lake it does."

"I like Sarah."

"I like her too. She'll never move to New York, though." She shot a look at Constance and was startled by the intensity of her gaze. "You know what's going in Wisconsin right now, don't you?"

"Yes, of course. We can talk politics later. What I really want to know is whether you're happy here."

She told her about the class on how to blog, attempting to make it sound important. "I'm giving another this coming week, and then I'm thinking about doing creative writing classes."

Constance looked out the window at the passing scenery. When they turned onto the access road, she said, "That's all good. You can put it on your résumé. May I give you a little stored up wisdom?"

"Of course."

"Don't get sidetracked and end up going nowhere."

They were parked in front of Hayley's home. "Have I gotten sidetracked?"

"I thought maybe so, that's why I'm here, but only you know that." She opened the door of the old truck and stepped out onto the sandy drive. Today she wore capris and sandals and a top that showed a hint of cleavage. Her hair was pulled back and tamed by a wide barrette.

Hayley's parents stood up to greet her. They were serving coffee cake and coffee on the deck. Sarah parked off the side of the road, and she and Kristina, who like Constance wore capris and sandals, followed the other two. Hayley introduced Kristina and Constance, who gave her parents beautiful smiles.

Her mom responded warmly, her dad looked vaguely perplexed. She guessed he must wonder why these women had come all this way to see his daughter. The bringing together of these two parts of her life made Hayley nervous, and she was glad when they walked over to Sarah's place, where Kate and Pat also were making coffee and had set out breakfast rolls.

Kate held the dog in check while introductions were made. When they all begged off any more food and drink, Pat suggested they go down to the lake. Beach chairs had been set out under the shade of a willow, but everyone walked past them to the water beyond.

"How lovely this is," Constance said, taking off her sandals and wading in.

As luck would have it, Eddie's Ski Nautique was one of the two speedboats zipping around the lake. He waved as he sped past. Hayley hoped he wouldn't stop, but of course on his next pass he cut the engine and idled up to the pier, throwing a rope around a post.

He hopped onto the planks and strode toward them. "I can't miss what might be the last nice day of the season. Hello, ladies." All heads were turned toward him. "Would you enjoy a ride around the lake?"

The dog rallied and met Eddie halfway, where he stuck his nose in Eddie's crotch in greeting. Hayley guffawed. She looked at Sarah, whose frown turned into a grin. Kate called Junior to her side.

"Well," Kristina said, glancing at Constance.

Hayley stepped up and introduced Eddie, who said, "I need

someone to drive the boat and someone to spot me when I ski. Or one of you can ski."

"I'd love to see one of you ski," Constance said. A warm breeze had freed a few hairs around her face and she held them back with a hand. Her eyes were hidden behind sunglasses.

"I'd like to try it," Kristina said.

"We must have a suit that will fit. Come with me," Kate said.

It all seemed surreal to Hayley. She looked at Sarah. "Let's go change."

That left Pat to entertain Constance and Eddie. When they came back, Constance was holding court on the pier, her bare feet dangling in the water. The other two seemed to be hanging on her words.

Everyone skied, except Kate and Constance, who sat together on the shore and watched. To Hayley's amazement, Kristina got up on the first try and was skiing on one ski by the end of the morning. Hayley and Pat skied together, enveloped in watery spray shot through with rainbows. Even Sarah skied on one ski. Pat drove the boat when Eddie showed off his acrobatic skills on the water.

Kate and Pat went inside to fix a late lunch. Sunburned and happy, they all ate sandwiches and snacked on grapes and chips and drank iced tea. Constance and Kristina were scheduled to fly out of the Outagamie Airport at five fifteen.

"We didn't take them to the fish hatchery," Hayley said to Sarah.

"Maybe next time," Sarah replied. "I heard Mom inviting them back."

"No shit?" She looked at Constance and Kate, who were in deep conversation, and thought they would make a great match. Pat was talking to Kristina, and Eddie looked kind of lonesome.

"None."

"Do you think Eddie knows how out of the loop he is?"

"I think he thinks he can charm anyone."

Hayley laughed.

After lunch, she and Sarah walked Constance and Kristina back to Hayley's house to say goodbye to her parents. Sarah drove them to the motel in Waushara where they'd left the rental car.

Hayley was quiet on the way home. The vitality the two women had brought with them was gone. The day lost some of its zest without them.

"They certainly were game for anything. I couldn't believe it when Kristina wanted to ski." Sarah said.

"I couldn't either. I'd forgotten how Constance brings a sort of energy everywhere she goes."

"You haven't gotten over her, have you?"

"Maybe you never do when someone dumps you."

"She could be your mother, Hayley." Sarah shot an indecipherable look at her.

"I told you that."

"You told me you had a crush on my mom too. At least Kristina is around our age."

"Constance told me not to get sidetracked."

"By what?"

"She didn't say. Thought maybe you could help me with that." She'd taken it as a warning not to get complacent about her job situation.

"Makes me think of a train on one of those tracks that go nowhere."

"Exactly. Is that what I'm doing, Sarah?" This was a risky question, knowing that Sarah wanted them to live together.

Sarah surprised her. "You know, I've been thinking about us. They say you shouldn't go from one person to another, like from Kristina to me."

Hayley asked, "Who is 'they'?"

"Therapists, people who give advice."

"Like your mom."

"She didn't say that, but she probably would."

Hayley knew this. "Well, I guess I'm doing the right thing, but maybe I need to find a place of my own."

She could almost see Sarah wince. "You probably should."

CHAPTER FOURTEEN

Fall 2011

September turned into October. The leaves began to turn in earnest. Sometimes she and Sarah fell asleep over their phones when talking at night. Hayley had looked at apartments, but they all wanted too much up front—a month's deposit, plus the final month, plus the present one. Nor could she really afford her health insurance, an expensive COBRA with a high deductible.

She blogged furiously, never questioning her increasingly indignant stance on the changes being made statewide. More than fifty thousand people would lose Badger-Care coverage and over two hundred thousand would be moved into programs with reduced benefits—programs funded by state and federal funds. The costs for those who lost coverage would fall ultimately on taxpayers.

However, concealed carry was the hot-button issue. Rules for concealed carry licenses had to be in place by November 1. City and county boards were scrambling to create ordinances to ban concealed carry in public buildings. The NRA was unhappy with the state attorney general's proposed weapons training rules that would require four hours of training. The governor said the rules could be changed later. *God forbid elected officials displease the NRA*, she wrote half in jest, pleased at what a difficult position this must put them in.

Over the weekend the maples glowed with bright colors—reds and oranges and yellows. Indian summer arrived on Tuesday, the third. Hayley gloried in it, knowing it would probably not get into the high seventies again until April rolled around and then only if they were lucky. She sat on the beach until the orb of bright sun slipped behind the tree line.

On Friday she looked up to see Sarah walking down the beach toward her. She wore a nice pair of slacks and a blouse and carried her shoes in one hand.

Hayley jumped to her feet and waited. When Sarah drew close, she said, "I know a nice little spot surrounded by white pines where no one can see us."

"Except Eddie," Sarah said, which would have spoiled the moment had she not smiled beatifically. "Where is this nice little spot exactly?"

"How about I show you? Did I tell you how good you look?"

"I know that old line. Good enough to eat." She lifted her hair off her neck, shook it out and smiled wryly. "Is that how I look?"

"That too." This was foreplay, she thought, itching to reach out to Sarah. They stood two feet apart, proscribed from any real public displays of affection.

"Well, what are we waiting for?"

She led Sarah to an opening in a small grove of trees. The sand was covered with a bed of needles. "Remember this place?"

"Of course. How could I forget?" She took Hayley's face between her hands and kissed her, then said, "I know I'm not as exciting as Constance or Kristina, but I'm here and ready to do your bidding."

"I think you're exciting. I can't wait to get into your pants." After chancing a look toward the lake, hidden by greenery, she fell to her knees, taking Sarah with her. She fumbled with Sarah's belt, unhooked it and the clasp and pulled the zipper down. First pressing her cool palm against Sarah's warm belly, she slid her fingers into the wiry pubic hair.

Sarah was still working on the buttons and zipper that held Hayley's capris up. "Let me catch up here," she said, her warm breath exhaling into Hayley's mouth.

She waited till she felt Sarah's touch before beginning the slow stroke that drove Sarah crazy. When Sarah moved urgently against her hand, she whispered. "I want to do it the other way, before it's too late."

"No," Sarah breathed. "This is too public."

And then she was lost in sensation too.

After, when she was once again conscious of the sights and sounds around her, she marveled at how everything disappeared into passion when they made love. Was it love? Neither said she loved the other, not even when desire overtook them. Love had become a casual word, one said at the end of a phone call.

She kissed Sarah hard. "I get so horny when you're gone."

Sarah said, "It's not quite the same, doing it to yourself, is it?"

"I'd like to see that sometime though. I think it would be a turn-on."

"Yeah, well, you're not going to. It's just too private." She returned the kiss. "Do peanut butter and jelly sandwiches sound good? Pat and Mom are going out for fish."

***

"You want a place of your own? I know someone who is looking for a live-in house watcher for a month," Hayley's dad said at supper Monday night.

"Who is that?" she asked, a forkful of mashed potatoes halfway to her mouth. He'd caught her by surprise, because she hadn't said anything about moving.

"Harry and Sally Bryzinski. Their place is down at the other end of the lake. We cleared his driveway. It's a pretty big house. They're going to visit family in California. You interested?"

"What does it entail?"

Her mom was looking from her to her father, a slight frown between her brows. "She just moved back in."

"I know, honey, but Harry asked if she'd consider staying there. He asked about her." He met Hayley's gaze. "It just means that you'd live there for the month that they're gone. Keeps burglars away. We had some break-ins around the lake during the winter months."

She moved in the day the Bryzinskis left. Their home was at least twice as big as the one she'd grown up in—two stories with a balcony that overlooked the living room. A huge satellite TV screen hung over a fireplace large enough for her to climb into. Rustic furniture filled the rooms. After hanging her clothes in one of the guest room closets and putting her folded stuff in the dresser, there was nothing to do except work on her blog.

The governor had frozen state workers' wages for two years and seized control of their work schedules. The twist on this was the governor had accepted a six thousand dollar raise voted for in the previous legislature, even after he'd said the financial playing field had to be leveled for everyone.

She segued into the continuing saga of state government's handling of concealed carry. After the NRA complained, a legislative committee dropped the four-hour required training class, angering even the Republican attorney general. After all, everyone had to learn how to drive a car before getting a driver's license. No concealed carry would be allowed in the senate gallery. However, in the assembly an observer could be arrested for taking pictures from the gallery but not for carrying a concealed weapon. Legislators would be allowed to carry weapons and to decide whether to allow guns in their offices, but there would be no metal detectors at the Capitol doors.

Her blog had turned into a much frequented website, not only for those who agreed with her but for those who didn't. She stared at the huge bank of windows that faced the lake. They were black with night. She could not see out, but anything or anyone could see in. There were no drapes or blinds to hide her, and she felt uncomfortably exposed. She remembered teasing Shirley when they left the bookstore that first night after class for feeling unsafe when she went out to her car at night. "This is Waushara, not New York City," she'd said, but that didn't mean there was no crime around here. Hadn't her dad said there had been break-ins in unoccupied cottages around the lake last winter?

It was the Friday before Halloween. When she became discouraged with the battle she'd taken on, Rachel Maddow's commentary about "The Great State of Wisconsin" lifted her up. Rachel was talking about Wisconsin when the doorbell rang.

Who the hell? Heart racing, she jumped off the couch. Sarah was coming on Saturday. She peered through the side windows next to the door and let out a little shriek when someone looked back at her. It was Eddie, his nose flattened and his mouth stretched open in a distorted grin. Annoyed by the scare, she said through the opening. "What do you want?"

"Trick or treat," he said.

"Ha, ha. I'm busy."

"Aw, come on. I brought some beer and a pizza."

It was the promise of pizza that convinced her to open the door. She'd had a frozen dinner for supper and was still hungry.

"Why are you here anyway?" she asked. "I thought you were working for a law firm in Milwaukee." They were sitting at the immense table in the dining area, next to the wall of windows that separated the wraparound deck from the dining and living area.

"Not anymore," he said, talking around a mouthful of pizza. "After they were through with the redistricting, they let me go."

"But that was months ago. What have you been doing since?"

"I do a lot of wills and powers of attorney and title searches and personal injury stuff. I've been busy. Got a little office in town."

"Here?" she asked with surprise. No wonder he kept showing up.

"Well, yeah. I like the area. I'm looking for a place to buy. Is this one for sale?" He grinned.

As if he could afford it. "Not as far as I know. How did you find me?"

"I've been following you," he said with a straight face.

"Come on, Eddie. That's not funny."

"Your dad told me." He took a slug of beer. "All we need is a fire." He grinned. "I brought some maryjane."

"Figures," she said. "You can't smoke in here."

"Let's sit out on the porch."

"It's goddamn cold." She popped the last bite of pizza in her mouth and wiped off her hands.

"Bundle up."

She was glad for the company, she realized. It was lonely here. She grabbed her winter jacket as he shrugged into his, and they went out the front door into the cloudy night. Huddled on the Adirondack chairs on the porch they watched rain fall. When Eddie passed the hand-rolled cigarette to her, she waved it away.

"The smell is making me high." She felt a little sad. "Why do you keep turning up, Eddie? Seriously? Why aren't you out with some available woman?"

"I haven't met someone I like as much as you and Sarah."

"Well, you aren't going to change us. You know that, don't you?"

"You don't want to have my baby? I thought every woman wanted a baby."

"Not this one. I don't have a regular job. I don't have my own place. Get real, Eddie."

"You could live with me when I find a place. I could use the money, and you wouldn't be home with Mummy and Daddy."

It was as if he'd prodded a wound, and she said indignantly, "Lots of college grads have moved back home out of necessity. They're not there because they want to be."

"Yeah, but you could have stayed with Sarah and you chose not to. You can live with me and have it both ways."

Appalled that he'd think she'd consider such a thing, she raised her voice. "What? You don't get it, Eddie. I don't want it with you." Apparently she had given him hope. "Get on with your life. I'm not looking for a man." Her heart was pounding for some stupid reason. Surely, after spying on her and Sarah, he knew she was a lesbian.

"You know who really likes you and Sarah? Mark Sorenson. You don't want him hanging around."

"You gotta be kidding. That was years ago when we went to Indian Crossing." Sometimes, though, he came to the gas station. "I don't want either one of you hanging around. Finish that thing. I want to go inside and light a fire in the fireplace."

He pinched the end of the shredding joint and put it in his pocket. "I'll build you a roaring fire. You'll see how useful I am."

She decided to let him do it. His remark about Mark unnerved her. What was to keep him from showing up? "Sorenson doesn't know I'm living here, does he?" she asked as Eddie built the fire— wadding up newspaper, adding fat wood, kindling and split oak.

"You can't keep a secret around here. Word gets out pretty fast. I should stay here and protect you."

Shivers climbed her spine at the thought of Sorenson showing up at her door some night. Who would hear her if she hollered for help? She put the poker within reach.

Eventually they both fell asleep in front of the blaze Eddie had built. An unexpected sound outside the windows startled them awake. A masked face was pressed against the glass. Hayley leaped to her feet and grabbed the poker.

Eddie said, "What? What's going on?" He peered at the face and jumped out of the chair, tripping on a rug. "Who is that?" But the face was gone.

The thought that she might not be able to stay here alone if strangers peered in the windows made Hayley angry, and she ran outside with the poker. She rounded the side of the house, stumbling down the steps to the driveway, as someone darted around the far corner of the house. She hoped Eddie had locked the door behind her.

She doubled back to the lake side of the house and caught sight of someone disappearing through the open door, but when she got to it, it was locked. She banged on the glass, yelling Eddie's name.

He opened the door. "How come it was locked?"

"'Cause whoever locked it just went in the house. Where have you been? You had to see him."

She slipped inside and latched the door. "Okay. Where is he?" The poker hung from her right hand.

"Who?" Eddie asked.

Then she saw a man in a knit facemask, standing behind Eddie, clutching a baseball bat. Her heart painfully tripped into high gear. "Watch out!"

The bat connected with Eddie's head, and he sort of crumpled as she watched in disbelief. New York City was dangerous, not this part of the country. This couldn't be happening to her. She clutched the poker with both hands and decided to go for the intruder's left arm, the one that held the baseball bat. Was Sorenson a leftie? She couldn't remember.

He took a step toward her. Instead of backing off, she moved forward and swung the poker as hard as she could. At the last moment he lurched backward but not quickly enough. He grabbed the bat with his right hand as his left wrist cracked. Then he swung and connected with her shoulder. She staggered under a flash of pain and almost landed in the fireplace. He stumbled toward her and she sidestepped, putting all her strength behind the poker, aiming for the same arm. Another crack. She ducked as the bat came her way, and black spots danced before her eyes.

Someone yelled, "Hey!" as the bat glanced off the side of her head. She felt herself falling.

She awoke as a kneeling man fastened a cervical collar around her neck. Two people loaded her onto a gurney. Her shoulder was killing her, not her neck, and she said so.

"You'll be all right. We're taking you to the hospital. Is there anyone we should call?"

"My parents," she said, giving him the number. "But you have to lock the doors. I'm house-sitting here, and someone just broke in." She tried to turn her head to look for Eddie and, of course, couldn't move it. "Where's Eddie? The guy hit him over the head with a baseball bat."

"He's in the ambulance already." The gurney rolled over the floor.

The cedar ceiling passed overhead. Then she was carried through the rain and slid into the ambulance. Her shoulder burned with pain. She felt dizzy. The yard was alight with red and blue flashing lights.

"That you, Hayley?" Eddie asked from somewhere beside her. "What happened? I've got the goddamnest headache."

She spoke to the ceiling of the ambulance. "Somebody hit you over the head with a baseball bat."

They began to move, rocking down the driveway, picking up speed when they hit the road. She felt as if she might fall off the gurney and tried to balance.

"It's okay," the EMT said from somewhere beside her. "We're just going around a curve." When the siren wailed, he reassured her. "We only turn the siren on when we go through stop signs or lights or pass someone."

A cuff had been attached to her good arm. The first time it tightened she started, and he'd told her, "It takes your blood pressure every few minutes."

Her parents met them at the hospital as she was being wheeled through the emergency doors. They walked alongside the gurney, only dropping away as she was taken to a room with an MRI. The doctor on call cleaned her head wound and put in a few stitches.

Her skull was not fractured, but she had suffered a concussion. Her shoulder was badly bruised and dislocated, but not broken. She was given pain medication and put in ICU, where her parents again reappeared.

"How is Eddie?" she asked.

"They took him to Theda Clark Hospital."

"Who hit us?" But she fell asleep before hearing any answer. She'd meant to ask them to call Kate so that she could tell Sarah.

The nurse came in during the night and took her vitals. There were only the two of them. She was disoriented, too dizzy to talk and quickly fell asleep again.

Saturday morning Sarah showed up. "I leave you alone for a few days and what happens?"

She smiled but was not quick-witted enough to come up with a retort. "Maybe you can tell me what happened."

"The guy in the ape mask was Herman Jablonski, and the guy who rescued you was Mark Sorenson. Who is this Jablonski anyway?"

Hayley frowned. Herman Jablonski was the guy in her blogging class who had been so keen about concealed carry. She supposed he'd had a gun hidden on him and shivered with cold.

She told Sarah about the blog. "Who would have thought Mark would be the good guy, though? You remember Sorenson, don't you?" She was thinking if he'd gotten there earlier, he might have been the bad guy.

"Do you forget someone who tries to rape you? Jablonski is charged with assault and breaking and entering, but he's out on bond."

"Maybe Sorenson planned to break in and Jablonski beat him to it. Dad said someone was breaking into lake homes last winter."

"Maybe you better not teach those classes."

"It has to be a coincidence." She hoped so anyway. "How's Eddie?"

"I hear he's holding his own. They thought his skull was fractured at first. That's why they took him to Theda Clark. But it was just a bad concussion."

She squeezed Sarah's hand. "I want out of here."

"Your mom says they'll probably let you go tomorrow. You have a huge lump on your head and a shoulder that must really ache."

Her arm was in a sling attached to her chest. Whenever she accidentally moved it, she screamed inwardly at the pain.

***

She moved back in the Bryzinski house the next week, after a few days at home. Having been notified of the assault and break-in, the owners had had cameras and motion detector lights installed around the outside of the house. The lights came on whenever something moved within their perimeters—a deer or raccoon or a branch swaying in the wind. The sudden glare was almost as alarming as the dark. But now the Bryzinskis were paying her to house-sit.

On Friday she was posting on her blog. The GOP-controlled senate was rushing legislation that would put the new districts in place immediately—in time for any recall elections that would take place next year, including the governor's. However, the lone GOP senator who had voted against the union-stripping bill said if he were recalled the constituents who put him in office should have a chance to vote him out of it. Because of his refusal to vote for it, the bill was dropped.

When she heard the knock, she hurried to let in Sarah, who was dancing in the cold light of a motion detector. She had told Hayley that she planned to spend every weekend with her, to keep her safe. No one had wanted Hayley to move back in the Bryzinski house, including herself, but the fact that the homeowners were now paying her gave weight to her decision.

She locked the door behind Sarah and gathered her in her good arm, kissing her cold face till she pulled away.

"What is it, Hayley?" she asked.

"Don't I always greet you like this?"

"Like it's the last time you're going to see me? No."

Coming face-to-face with someone who seemed keen on killing her had humbled and scared Hayley. "I've got a fire going. It makes the rest of the place cold, so keep your jacket handy."

Her laptop sat open on the coffee table in front of the large couch. Antlers held up the back cushions. A pulsing fire leaped in the grate, blue and red and crackling. Hayley had stacked wood on the hearth, so she wouldn't have to go outside to get it. She wanted to minimize the danger of another assault. She didn't trust Mark Sorenson. When the sheriff asked him why he was there, he claimed he was following Jablonski because he knew he was breaking into empty summer homes around the lakes. He'd said Jablonski sometimes stayed in them.

They sat on the couch, staring at the flames, not touching because someone might be watching through the bank of windows. "Why don't they have any window coverings?" Sarah asked.

"If anyone was out there, the motion detector lights would be on. I don't know how far out they go, though." Someone could be standing out of range. It made her uneasy.

"They sent Eddie home. He'd been released when I called the hospital last. He could even be back here."

"A lot of help he was." She pictured him going down in slow motion.

"That slimeball, Mark Sorenson, saved you."

She looked out the windows, blank against the night. "Let's turn off the lights." No one could see them then. When the room was dark, they sat down again.

It had been a lovely day—high fifties and sunny. When their eyes adjusted, the lake and sky became visible through the trees. Light from a half moon shimmered on the water. Pinpoints of stars popped out, also reflected in the lake's surface.

Hayley poured them each a glass of Shiraz. She put her uninjured arm around Sarah who scooted closer. Hayley's attitude had changed since the assault last Friday. She no longer felt she had years to play around. Anyway, whom was she going to play with? She was probably never going back to New York.

"I was so scared when Mom called and told me you were in the hospital and terrified when I found out what happened," Sarah said quietly. "Do you have insurance?"

"I have a COBRA I can't really afford." How much longer would that last?

"I didn't care about anything else when I found out you'd been hurt—not Eddie and his spying on us, not your moving back home or into this house. All that mattered was that you were alive and safe."

Hayley leaned forward. "Let's bank the fire and hit the sack." She shut the flames behind the glass doors and took Sarah's hand.

When they were huddled under the goose down blanket in the guest room, warm skin pressed against warm skin, idly caressing each other's backs, Hayley said. "You know what my first thought was when I came to?"

"My left shoulder blade," Sarah said. Hayley scratched the spot. "What?"

"That we might never do this again." Actually, that thought came after she realized she was safe and alive.

Later, when she was lying on her back, looking at the fan on the ceiling, the room suddenly lit up. She jumped out of bed, heart and head pounding, and crawled to the window. At least there were blinds in the bedrooms. She lifted the bottom of one and peered out. Three young deer, probably this year's babies, stood frozen in the glare.

Sarah knelt at her side. Shoulder to shoulder, they watched

the deer bolt into the safety of darkness. "That's scary when those lights go on. How can you stay here?"

"I have to. I need the money and besides, I can't let fear rule my life." As she said it, she knew that's what she'd been doing. She'd feared commitment. She hadn't wanted to answer to anyone—with her money, with her choice of friends, with her time. Now it didn't seem to matter much. This was not how she wanted to spend the rest of her life—living in someone else's house, working at a gas station.

"I think it's foolish to stay here after what happened. You're a target."

"I won't be here much longer. Just till the end of the month." Shivering, they climbed back in bed. "Should we give it a go? Living together?"

Sarah took her hand. "I don't want you back if you don't want to be there. I actually mean that."

CHAPTER FIFTEEN

Fall 2011

When Jenkins reduced her hours the next week, she knew she'd have to find another job if only to pay her health insurance. She turned to the web—writing ad content and political articles, picking up more advertisements for her blog. It was time consuming, often challenging and sometimes boring. She quickly realized it wouldn't pay her way and sought a job at one of the newspapers in the Fox Valley.

She was eating at her parents' home on a Sunday night when her mom suggested she go back to school for her master's degree.

She stared at her. "I can't afford it. Besides, it's no guarantee of a job these days."

Her father cleared his throat. "We can help."

She'd been annoyingly emotional since being hit by the baseball bat and covered her eyes with a hand to hide unexpected tears.

Her mother touched her arm. "It's just that you've had such bad luck. We didn't have to help much when you went to Brown."

She cleared her throat and said, "Do you even know how much it will cost?"

"Yes. What better way to invest?" her father said with an ironic smile.

"You could live with Sarah and go to UW-Oshkosh," her mom said.

"Or go to the Tech and be a web designer," her dad added.

She wiped her nose on a paper napkin and tried to smile. "I'll look into it. Thanks. Do you know how cool you are?"

"About time you found that out," her dad mumbled.

She told Sarah about this conversation on the phone that night, while snuggled under the down blanket they had shared over the weekend. "What do you think? Oshkosh or the Tech?"

Sarah was slow in answering. "Only you can decide that. Sure you want to move in with me?"

"Only if I can pay my share. I'm making some money on the web, but I can't move until the end of the year. Are you sure you still want me?"

"Yes, yes, yes. But I'm a jealous person. I won't share you."

"I can't have friends?"

"Friends, yes. Lovers, no."

"Just so that criterion is mutual." She smiled. "Listen. We need to talk about it. What if I don't find a job in the Fox Cities?"

"You will, and you make money off web writing and your blog."

"Not near as much as you make."

"Here's your chance to do what you want to do. Whatever you make will be enough."

Hayley chose to believe her. "I love you, babe."

"I love you too. It's been a long time since we said that."

"Well, you can't be flinging it around all the time like an afterthought."

***

The newspaper in the Fox Cities hired her as their webmaster, succeeding someone who was leaving after the first of the year for a similar position in Milwaukee. She had not expected to land the job and was thrilled and a little nervous. She also made inquiries about starting a how-to-blog class at the Tech, but it was too late for the next semester. It was also late to register for classes at either the Tech or UW-O. Besides, she felt she would have to give the newspaper job her full attention. Nor could she afford to neglect her blog.

Even though she had Sunday, Monday and Tuesday off now, she couldn't spend those days at Sarah's apartment. She was stuck at the Bryzinski place till their return at the end of November. After giving notice at Jenkins's for Friday, December 16, she was chafing for that day to arrive and sent some of her stuff home with Sarah.

She had plenty to blog about, though. The state had been bleeding jobs for months. In October, Wisconsin had led the nation with 9,700 job losses—9,300 of which were in the private sector. This happened after the governor held his "jobs session" with the legislature during which no actual jobs bills were even taken up.

On November 5 a committee, formed by one of the governor's own supporters, had filed a recall petition with the State Government Accountability Board under the name of "Close Friends to Recall Walker." The recall effort against the governor was set to begin November 15. A kick-off rally in Madison had been scheduled for Saturday, the 19th. The sixty days that were allowed for collecting over 540,000 signatures would still begin on the 15th. However, as of the November 5th filing, the governor could begin amassing unlimited amounts of campaign funds. Hayley blogged heatedly about how unfair this was.

On November 15 Hayley's mom and dad printed and signed their names, filled out their addresses and dated recall petitions for the governor and lieutenant governor that Hayley had downloaded from the web.

"I want one of those to take to work," her dad said, and Hayley promised to print a couple for each of them.

"If you want more, we can download them anytime."

She knew from Sarah that Pat had left for Oshkosh to work in their recall office. Hayley went to Kate's house when she left her own.

Kate signed the petition at the kitchen counter. "Be prepared to meet a lot of opposition. This is a conservative county. You'll have better luck in the Fox Cities." She handed the papers back to Hayley and met her eyes. "It's about time you and Sarah moved in together. If any two people belong together, you do. You've been best friends since you were little kids. That's a great foundation for a relationship."

"Thanks. Can I call you Mom-in-law now?" Hayley said with a grin.

"Any time." Kate's smile lit up her eyes. "Did you hear on WPR this morning that the polls are with us?"

She hadn't but said, "Exciting, isn't it."

"Think we'll get enough signatures?"

"We have to."

"I am so glad we're doing something like this, instead of just complaining."

"Yeah, me too. What does Pat think?"

"She feels the same. We'll have a better idea about its success in a week or two."

"I better go," Hayley said, although she wanted to stay. "Thanks for signing."

Since she couldn't go to Madison for the kickoff rally, Sarah spent the weekend with her. They made rounds of the lake residents, managing to fill one recall page each—one for the governor and one for the lieutenant governor. Most lake homes were closed for the winter. After, they went back to Bryzinskis', lit a fire and watched Badger football on the giant TV screen. It was a great year to be a football fan in Wisconsin.

"You know what?" Hayley said as they sprawled on the immense couch. "I don't want to go back to New York. I understand now why you felt you had to stay here."

"Do you?" Sarah's face was in shadow. The only light in

the room came from the flickering TV and the fire that blazed underneath it.

"Trying to turn the tide here gets hold of you and won't let go."

"Everything is at stake, including our lake. They'd do away with all the environmental protections in exchange for a few jobs. I'll never understand that. Tourism is big business here. It creates jobs."

"It's hard to track how many, though. You don't have to get on your soapbox for me. Now that we're all awake and aware it's almost too late. I never would have come back had you not been here." Which meant she never would have really appreciated her parents or where she grew up. "So, thanks."

"I love you, Baxter." Sarah's teeth glimmered briefly. "I always have."

"No one calls me Baxter." She laughed, remembering the day they'd inadvertently run into each other in the Capitol. "I couldn't love you more, Sarah."

***

On December 15, a month after the recall began, 507,000 signatures had been gathered. Hayley and Sarah stood on the pavement outside the public library the following Saturday, clipboards in hand. In November Wisconsin again had the highest job loss of any state in the nation. The library had proved to be a fertile place for collecting signatures.

Sarah's mom stayed with Sarah during the week so that she could work in the recall office. Dogs were allowed in Sarah's apartment complex. No dogs were permitted where Pat bunked with her friend in Oshkosh. Two more bodies in the few rooms had made space tight and now that Hayley had moved in, they'd no doubt be bumping into each other. However, Hayley was looking forward to having Kate around. On weekends Kate went home, which would give them time for privacy.

The weather was unusually warm, but standing outside on pavement in thirty degree temperatures eventually chilled the bones. Sarah's cheeks and nose were ruddy. Hayley asked, "What do you want for Christmas?"

"You keep asking me that," Sarah said.

"And you never answer," Hayley replied as two people came out of the library and walked up to them. "Did you want to sign the petitions?"

"You bet," the gray-haired man said. "We thought you'd come door to door."

She gave him the clipboard with the petition for the recall of the governor on one side and the lieutenant governor on the other and told him how to fill out the lines. "Nope. We're all over the place, but we're not going door to door for this. Too time consuming."

The woman, who was signing Sarah's petitions, said, "We saw some people with signs out on West College. People were driving into a vacant parking lot and signing, but we didn't know if they were legitimate." There had been cause to worry that the opposition was also collecting signatures and throwing them away. Kate had told Sarah that was why so many came into the office to sign.

"They were our people," Sarah said with a smile. "Hey, thanks for doing this."

"Thank *you*. You're the ones out here in the cold," the man said, handing back the clipboard.

The sun had slipped behind buildings, taking the temperatures down with it.

"Let's go soon. Okay? I'm cold and it's getting dark."

On the way back to the recall office, Hayley said, "There's little time to shop." She really disliked shopping.

"I'd rather have signatures. You know, at the beginning of this I was worried. Now I'm just amazed at the number of people wanting to sign. Besides, you don't have any money. You have to buy a car."

"That was one thing I didn't need in New York," Hayley said. She was still driving her dad's old truck.

Sarah said, "Let's just fill stockings. I'll get something for Mom and Pat and Beth's baby, and you get something for your parents and Mike. Maybe we better go shopping tomorrow. I've got a thirty percent off coupon at Kohl's."

"Where are we going to spend Christmas?" Hayley said. "That's the big question."

"I've had some thoughts." Sarah pulled into a parking space near the recall office.

Inside, three people sat behind tables. Only one person was paid to oversee each of the offices around the state. Their guy was young. His boss was young. Both college graduates. All the others—those who worked at the recall offices and those who stood outside cafés and libraries and other public places—were volunteers.

They signed and turned their petitions in to a woman behind one of the desks and waited while she looked them over.

"Have a lot of people been in to sign?" Sarah asked.

"It's been steady. You two got a lot of signatures."

"We were at the library. See you on Monday," She double-checked to see that her name was on the volunteer sheet taped to the wall.

Back in the car, Sarah said. "Let's spend Christmas Eve morning and evening with your parents and Christmas Day with Mom and Pat."

"We'll have to go to church Christmas Eve, you know."

Sarah shrugged. "That's okay with me."

Hayley knew this was a better arrangement than many gay couples had. Often they went separately to their respective families for holidays. "Let's buy presents together or at least say they're from both of us."

The dark and empty apartment greeted them. There were leftovers, though, that would hold them till Kate returned Monday morning. Hayley shrugged out of her heavy jacket and went straight to the fridge, turning on lights as she went. "Pat goes home on weekends, doesn't she?"

"Do you think something has gone wrong between them? Pat was away much of the summer too."

"She was getting signatures. Do you want her to move in with us too?"

"I don't want Mom to be alone."

"Isn't that why your mom goes home on weekends? Want a beer?"

"I hope so and yes."

Sarah turned on the TV and searched for news. No football. The Badgers were headed to the Rose Bowl. No news either. "Damn, I wish something was on Saturday night."

Hayley handed her a Leinie's Red. "I'm not entertainment enough anymore?"

"Of course you are. I've got homework to grade anyway."

"I'll heat up dinner. I'm glad your mom lives here during the week."

Sarah gave her a wet kiss. "I think you love my mom as much as you do me."

"Only when she cooks," Hayley said.

***

A thin layer of snow covered the ground at Christmas. Hayley had been hoping for a big snow dump once they got to the lake. Her parents had cut a tree. It stood in front of the bay window in the living room, brightly lit and hung with all the decorations that she and Mike had made when they were kids along with those accumulated through the years.

When she opened her bedroom door, she was surprised by a double bed where the bunk beds had once been. Her mother stood behind her, peering over her shoulder.

"Is it big enough?" she asked, and Hayley threw her arms around her. She and Sarah wouldn't have to squeeze into the bottom bunk.

"Thanks, Mom." She spied her dad hovering nearby. "You too, Dad."

Sarah was already in the room, running her hand over the quilt. "Nice," she said.

The next morning after breakfast and opening gifts, they moved on to see Kate and Pat, who, it turned out, had invited Hayley's parents for dinner.

While setting the table, Hayley overheard Sarah ask her mother if everything was all right.

"Why wouldn't it be all right?" Kate said with some asperity.

"Why does Pat have to go outside to talk to someone?" They could see Pat, phone to ear, hunched in a jacket while Junior nosed around the trees.

"Maybe she's calling her family."

Sarah turned away and Hayley took plates to the table on the porch. The lake with its layer of ice looked gray and cold and uninviting under a cloudy sky. She was standing in front of the windows, hugging herself, when Sarah put her arms around her.

"Hey, babe, what do you think?" Sarah whispered in her ear.

"If something's wrong, you'll find out soon enough."

"In other words, mind my own business."

Hayley put her hands over Sarah's encircling arms. "Your mother does."

"I'm just worried."

"I know. You need to let it go."

Sarah let Hayley go and went back to the kitchen.

Hayley studied the lake, trying to remember the warmth of summer. She heard Pat and the dog come in the side door. The dog's nails skittered across the floor.

Pat asked, "What can I do to help?"

And then Hayley's parents and Mike were at the door, her mom saying, "Are we too early?"

She turned and greeted them with hugs.

"We're going to get enough signatures, sis," Mike said as she put her arms around him.

"I think we've already got enough, don't you? From now on it's icing on the cake." She leaned back and looked up at him. Her scrawny little brother was at least six feet tall. She tried to put both hands around his bicep. "Where'd you get all the muscle?" He'd been a quarterback in high school. The Packers were playing that day. They would all watch, of course.

"Shearing Christmas trees." He winked at Sarah and gave her a hug.

"I think we all need a congratulatory drink," Kate said. "I've got a couple of bottles of champagne here. Let's pop some corks."

***

When Sarah and Hayley drove back to the Fox Cities the day after Christmas, Pat was still at the lake with Kate. They would be there till the day after New Year's, when Pat would go back to Oshkosh and Kate to the Fox Cities.

"Do you realize we're going to have to cook this week?" Hayley said.

Sarah grinned at her. "It'll be good to have some time alone. What are we going to do with it?"

"Get signatures. The question is what are we going to do in our spare time when we're through collecting signatures."

"Besides working regular jobs? Getting voters registered for the upcoming primaries and recall election?" Sarah added, "Do you think we've forgotten how to have fun?"

"Depends on your definition of fun." Hayley felt a twinge of panic over the new job.

She could not have pinpointed exactly when she began to feel positive about her move back home. The new job at the newspaper had renewed her self-confidence. It would be a challenge, though. The attack on her and Eddie at the Bryzinski place had made her realize she could be struck down any time, that it was foolish to take anything for granted. Her parents' forgiveness for her long absence and their acceptance of Sarah had filled her with gratitude. She knew she was fortunate—to have Sarah, to have a job, to be doing something she felt passionate about.

They fell asleep in each other's arms that night, in the middle of a kiss. Sometime during the dark hours, Hayley woke up feeling the cold of separation. She rolled toward Sarah and pulled her close. Life is good, she thought, and briefly wondered why it had taken her so long to get to this place, but then she drifted off.

***

On Tuesday, January 17, 2012, 1.9 million signatures were delivered to the Government Accountability Office in Madison. Nearly one million of those signatures were to recall the governor. Friday, the 13th, had been the last day to sign at recall offices around the state. That Friday evening Hayley and Sarah had attended a party for volunteers in their recall office. Even the food came from the volunteers. They were not going to the party at the Monona Terrace on the 17th. They both had to work the next day.

Instead, they held their own celebration on the 17th, drinking a couple of beers and eating popcorn as they watched MSNBC and Ed Schultz at Monona Terrace.

"Who would have thought?" Hayley said. "I was worried at first."

"So was I until we got over 300,000 signatures those first ten days."

Sarah's phone rang. They had already talked to Kate and Pat and Hayley's parents and Mike, proverbially slapping each other on the back. Brook had called earlier to say she was proud of them and almost ready to move back to Madison. Sarah picked up the phone and looked at the display and then at Hayley.

"Eddie. Should I answer?"

"Sure. I'm all in favor of crowing." Secretly, she had hoped it would be Constance. Did Constance even know? She seldom watched the tube.

Eddie had bought some land and was having a house built across from the lake access road. He and his boat would be a fixture on the lake again. "Want to go out to dinner this weekend? I'll be in town and I'll buy." Sarah held the phone near both her and Hayley's ears.

"What's the occasion?" Hayley said.

"Why, your big win, of course. And I want to introduce you to the new woman in my life."

"Anyone we know?" Sarah asked. "Where did you meet her?"

"She was the one collecting signatures when I signed the recall petitions."

They both laughed till Eddie sounded annoyed. "What's so funny? I thought you'd be happy about that."

"Why did you sign, Eddie?" Hayley asked.

"She was pretty. I wanted to meet her."

After they ended the call, they looked at each other and collapsed again in laughter. When she could speak, Sarah said, "Some things never change."

"Yeah, like us. We're hopelessly linked by the past, the present, the future."

Not really, she thought. Had things turned out differently in New York, she might still be there, and she would have missed these past eleven months. Coming home had been the best move she'd ever made.

"Think so?" Sarah gave her a smacking kiss that tasted of beer and popcorn.

"Absolutely."